I unlatched the sliding door that led from the loft onto the upper balcony, and stepped out into the breeze. Leaning against the rail, I looked down over the oily blackness of the ocean and the dim shimmering of the sand. It was all so peaceful and serene. Like eternity.

Then I saw a figure walking toward the water, a lithe woman, with flowing black hair and white skin, nude. She turned and beckoned to me, then waded out into the water.

I stared. There was no mistaking her, not from this distance.

It was Caroline.

A Wild Sea

Rebecca Montague

Cape Winds Press, Inc.
2000

Printed in the United States of America on acid-free paper
First Edition

ISBN 0-9671203-2-2

Library of Congress Number: 99-90869

Published by Cape Winds Press, Inc.
P.O. Box 730428
Ormond Beach, FL 32173-0428
http://www.capewindspress.com

Cover design by Mary Boone incorporating images obtained from IMSI's MasterClips/MasterPhotos© Collection, 1895 Francisco Blvd. East, San Rafael, CA 94901-5506, USA

To Jo. Just because.

I.

"Will you stop staring at that damned photograph?" I looked up at Mel and frowned. The memory fluttered once at the fringes of my mind and vanished, replaced by the low hum of the ferry engine.

We had the lower cabin of the small ferry alone to ourselves, the other twenty-odd passengers having chosen to enjoy the warm North Carolina day on deck during the crossing from the mainland to the island.

"Sorry." Sighing, I glanced again at the faded snapshot in my wallet, traced a finger across the vinyl separating me from Caroline's image, and closed the billfold. Leaning back, I transferred my gaze out the window over the choppy water. Across the Cape Fear River, I could see the lighthouse that marked our destination.

"You've been staring at that thing for an hour. Am I going to have to put up with this the entire trip?"

"Sorry," I said again, mechanically. I wasn't, really. I wanted to keep staring at the photo. The sound of the ferry engine vibrating beneath my feet reminded me of Caroline. It sounded much like the lower strings of an acoustic guitar being strummed in continuous rhythm. "I used to like to sit on the deck and listen to Caroline play her guitar," I commented almost absently.

"That was a long time ago, Kate." I looked over at my friend and smiled wanly.

"But I remember it like it was last night." It was so easy to remember. The sticky night air, the waves in the background breaking in syncopation with the gentle strains of her classically trained fingers on the strings of the Gibson.

I can still remember the way the beer bottle felt in my hand, cool and wet, the way the stars gleamed above and the katydids joined in chorus with the *'Recuerdos de la Alhambra'*. Caroline would sit there with her dark hair streaming down her back, oblivious to the humid night, her eyes bright as she serenaded me.

"Fifteen years is a long time to grieve, Katherine." Mel was giving me her counselor's eye. "Or to refuse to grieve, as the case may be. Are you sure you're ready to come back to where she died?"

I laughed bitterly. "I have no choice. You know it seemed in those days that we were immortal. Just one last year of college and our dreams would unfold, and we'd have our freedom. We'd have each other."

"You were a romantic in those days. We all were at that age, I think."

I looked at her and shook my head. "We weren't romantics. We were fools."

There was a silence. Finally I glanced up and saw the faint tinge of green to Mel's face. I couldn't help but grin at her. "Not feeling so well?"

"How did I ever let you talk me into this, Kate?" Melissa, born and raised in Nebraska, didn't do well on boats. I had only gotten her out on mine at the lake once, and she had spent the entire afternoon hanging over the edge feeding the fish.

I shrugged. "You didn't trust me coming alone?"

"Frankly, no. I still don't see why you had to come all the way back here. You could have handled the house from Seattle."

I pondered her comments, unsure myself why I had come. After fifteen years, what need had I for one last summer in the house that held such terrible memories? "I wanted to see it one more time," I replied, a little lamely.

"Caroline's long dead, hon. She's not going to be waiting for you at the dock."

Sharply, I glared at her. Then dropped my gaze and stared at the closed billfold in my hands. Could it be that I still couldn't accept the reality of what had happened, that somehow I expected to arrive and find her waiting for me with her hair blowing in the breeze and a smile on her brown lips?

No.

Caroline was dead, drowned fifteen summers past. Not even her ghost remained on Smith Island to haunt me, not after so many years. She died in her carefree way, and I have lived with the memory clawing at me for so long that I no longer cry when I come shaking from the nightmare recreation of the event into the darkness of my room. I was sure I had stopped blaming myself long ago. I stopped when I interred the last of my näivete along with my youth and settled into the quiet, respectable life that I now wore like a faded pair of jeans.

"I know. But I spent a lot of happy summers on Smith Island, a lot of happy time in that house. And now there's no choice but to tear it down. I want to say goodbye."

Years of erosion had eaten away at the land between the sea and our lot until the high tide broke within feet of the stairs. My father had intended to move the house to a new lot farther away from the ocean, but his death had finished any plan for that. I had no use for a summer house so far from home, and moving it to safety was too expensive a proposition for anyone to want to buy it. So, the relentless sea would claim another victim.

This time, I wouldn't cry.

"The house isn't the only thing you should say goodbye to while you're here." Mel's voice was soft. But if she hadn't been my best friend, I probably would still have slapped her.

"I've told you. Caroline died because of me. Because I was stupid. I can't just forget that. But I've gotten over it." I had repeated those last four words so often in the past decade and a half that I almost believed them. "Now please, can we change the subject?"

"You brought it up, Katherine."

The sound of the engine changed. Looking up, I realized we were passing through the channel into the marina of the island. With a sigh of relief, I stood up.

"Grab your bags. We're here."

Even though I hadn't been back in years, my father had kept me painfully abreast of changes to the island. As we gathered our bags and met the tram for the ride to the house, I had a moment to reflect that things had changed since my last visit. There was a new ferry terminal, a huge building which also housed a restaurant, chandler's and the corporate offices of the development company which owned the island. It was busier, too. The parking lot was filled with golf carts, the sole means of transportation on the island. Indeed, much changed from the half-deserted place Caroline and I had wandered over fourteen years earlier. The island had become 'popular', I suppose.

As the tram wove through the arbor of oak and palmetto trees along the main road, I counted the houses that I remembered: they were few compared to the new construction. I knew from my father that there had actually been a new house on the lot in front of ours, the beachfront lot, constructed two summers after my last visit. It had been lost to the horrendous erosion only four years after construction, during a hurricane that simply ripped the beach out from underneath it. And now what had once been our modest second row house was first row and counting. Next year the foundation would be first row for the fish.

There were condominiums flanking the newly erected clubhouse for the Smith Island Golf Club, also facing some danger from the erosion. I found some small satisfaction in seeing the efforts of man so handily dealt with by nature. I loved the island most when it had but the barest rudiments of a golf course and only eighteen houses with generator electric and propane lights. That was long ago and probably not remembered by many.

We had first started summering at Smith Island in 1978, when I was thirteen. One of my father's friends, an advertising executive from High Point, was the chairman of the board of the corporation that had started developing the island, and he talked my parents into spending a couple of weeks on the island with him and his wife.

I fell in love with the place immediately. Back then, we had jeeps to drive around in, and it was like having our own private estate. I wandered endless beaches without seeing another living soul. It was the happiest two weeks of my life. My parents fell in love with it as well, and we went back every summer thereafter, finally building, in 1981, the house Mel and I were going to stay at.

I had a lot of memories about the house. My mother spent her final summers there, where she was always happiest. I learned about astronomy from a neighbor who had a small observatory on his roof. Caroline and I spent many happy hours together there.

I glanced across at Mel, hoping she wouldn't be offended at my silence. We usually keep a running gab going, but I wasn't in much of a mood to talk. Melissa, obviously glad to be back on dry land, was too busy taking in the sights to question me about anything, which was fine. I could give her a tour later.

The tram deposited us at the back steps with our pile of luggage and groceries and puttered off with its load of smiling, tanned vacationers and their smiling, tanned children. I was glad to see them go. At least I would get a few hours of peace before everyone figured out I was here. I knew society on the island had its own rules and structure, and accepted that I would be expected to make the rounds to the various cocktail parties and social hours that my parents' friends would be giving, but I was not looking forward to it.

For one thing, I only drink with meals, rarely socially.

For another I can't stand feeling like a slave at auction, which is how I invariably feel when someone discovers that I'm single and starts trying to fix me up. It was irritating when I was twenty-five; now that I'm in my mid thirties it drives me insane. It doesn't matter what the setting is, someone starts trying to solve my 'problem'.

I've been at dinners where I've had two different men vying to impress me with their portfolios and cars and vital statistics and all I've wanted to do is stand up and scream, "Leave me alone!"

After the luggage was upstairs and put away and I had Melissa putting the groceries in the cupboards, I got a Coke out of the cooler, pulled back the curtains and stepped through the sliding glass door out onto the deck. It brought a shudder to me, and not just due to the wind whipping in from the sea.

I crossed to the railing and looked down at the beach. It was low tide, and the sand was dotted with sunbathers and children. No one was daring the surf; it churned in loud sprays of foam, driven by the wind. I closed my eyes, listened to the seagulls and remembered the way the dunes used to stretch out before the house; you couldn't see the beach then, expect from the little balcony deck at the very top of the house. A wooden walkway, darkened by exposure to the sun and salt, had wound from the deck over the dunes to the beach. The walkway was gone, the dunes were gone, and now a set of stairs led directly to the beach.

Caroline's face swam into my memory and I opened my eyes again. Melissa moved through the door behind me and joined me at the rail.

"Wow! You weren't kidding about the erosion, were you?" I shook my head. "Too bad; this is a neat house. Mind if I take a walk and explore a bit?"

"Go ahead. I've got to plug in the charger and get the carts running." Melissa nodded at me and kicked off her Birkenstocks before heading off down the stairs to the beach.

I watched her walk away before turning to go back through the house and down to the garage. The main part of the house was set ten feet up on posts which were sunk a good fifteen feet deep in the sand. The only enclosed part underneath was the garage. Behind it was a partially enclosed outdoor shower for washing off after swimming. A wooden slat walkway ran from the asphalt driveway around the garage to the shower and the to the foot of the front steps. Shells were scattered in the sand underneath the house.

Pulling the double doors open, I stepped inside and reached for the light switch. It looked remarkably unchanged to me. The two golf carts were new, the ones I remembered having been replaced long before.

But my father's extra set of golf clubs still leaned in the corner next to the umbrella for the deck table. The pegboard affixed to the back wall held its neat array of fishing poles, nets, crab pots, and beach chairs. Against the wall to my right stood the washer and dryer, next to the hot water heater. A pair of three speed beach bikes hung upside down from the joists. A shelf held plastic buckets and shovels, diving masks and snorkels, a metal detector, kneeboard, and three tackle boxes.

I knew that one of the boxes held fresh water tackle, the second surf-fishing tackle and the third, larger one, deep-sea tackle. The chargers for the golf carts were in the closet and it took me a few minutes to get them set up properly. When they were humming away, I stepped out into the sunlight and looked across under the house at the water.

I love the ocean. I always have. I spend several weeks a year on the Washington coast, where I have my own modest bungalow. But the Northwest coast isn't the same as the Southern coast. It never gets as hot or humid, the sun never seems quite as bright, and the air doesn't smell the same. Not being at Smith at all had been one of the most difficult things I had ever done. Not ever coming back would be the most difficult. Well, the second most difficult. I mounted the stairs slowly and went back inside.

Melissa came back to find me on the computer. The CNBC ticker ran on the television and I was making notes about the market close. She rolled her eyes at me and went to get a beer.

"Workaholic." She mouthed as she went past. I stuck my tongue out and punched a couple of keys on the computer. The printer came to life, spewing closing data for me. After making a few more notes, I went offline.

Melissa shook her head and lounged against the counter. "Did you pack your three piece business bikini?"

"I told you this was a working vacation. I'm in the market pretty heavily and I need to stay on top of it."

"Day trader."

I took the insult with appropriate humor. Melissa had always thought it was amusing that I spent so much time on the stock market, considering that we were both trained to be psychologists. She was finishing up her Doctoral thesis and I had dropped out after my father's death in order to manage his estate, which had dragged me into the world of market analysis. To my surprise, I liked it.

Melissa hadn't complained too much when I gave up my half of our fledgling practice to follow the market full time; after all, she had inherited my client base, and it was making her twice as much money.

"Did you enjoy your walk?"

"Yeah. There are some gorgeous women on this island." I shrugged.

"And I'd lay odds we're the only two women who care. Don't forget where we are."

"I know, but it doesn't hurt to dream."

My reply was curtailed by a 'yoo-hoo' from the deck. "Lord, it's begun already." I headed that way and met the woman at the door. "Why, hello Mrs. Millikan."

"Katie Jenkins! I knew it was you. Look at how you've changed! Why it's been years." I invited her in and offered her a drink. She took a Bloody Mary and, having introduced the two, I dispatched Melissa to fix it, since I invariably mess that sort of thing up. I knew there would be plenty of liquor in the bar - my father did a good job of drinking himself to death.

I know the official cause of his death was coronary thrombosis, but I also know that the real cause was the alcohol, and the alcohol was the result of a broken heart. He lost mother the year after I lost Caroline, and for a while it looked like the pair of us would end up roommates at an alcohol rehab center.

Fortunately, I was able to pull myself together and, in true family spirit, sank myself body and soul into my work. Dad turned to his work as well, but the bottle was never too far away. Other than his drinking, I've always admired my father and tried to be like him. As far as working myself half to death, I've succeeded.

Mrs. Millikan settled her madras plaid Bermuda shorts on the sofa and smiled through her tan at me – how did she stay so dark? "I heard from Jane Eder that you were coming for the summer. It's perfectly splendid; ever since you moved to Seattle we never see you any more. And how are you?"

Melissa plopped down in a chair and grinned at me. I'd tried to warn her about the type of southern women she would be meeting, but this was her first real experience with one of them.

"I'm fine," I answered, sipping at my Coke. "I appreciated your card after daddy passed away. There were so many things to do I'm afraid I didn't do a good job to responding to all of them."

She waved her hand in dismissal. "Oh, I never expected you to write back. Your father was so well-liked there must have just been bags of cards. But enough of that. I'm having social hour tonight at the villa from seven to eight and then I believe Margie Caldwell is having a little get-together – she'll just love to see you again. Did you bring your clubs? Oh, I see them there. My daughter Angela is here; you two must get together for a round, oh; do you play Melissa?"

"Golf? No, I'm afraid not."

"Too bad. Well, anyway, you remember where we are, Katie dear? Villa fourteen, on the end. I'll see both of you then? Wonderful to see you. Ta!" With a final swallow she was gone again and I collapsed into the sofa feeling as if I had just been struck by hurricane Millikan.

Melissa waited until she was certain the woman was gone, then burst out laughing. "Who was that whirlwind?"

"Janie Millikan, one of my mother's dearest friends. Oh, god, I'm doomed." I could see another reason why my father drank so much. It was tempting, just to survive the social hour. But I knew all about me and alcohol. I didn't dare break my oath to myself and start drinking like that again.

"Well, I'll start dinner if you want to take a shower or something."

"I think I'll take a stroll. It's either that or repeated head-banging."

Melissa snorted something in French and I went out toward the ocean. The tide was coming in, and I watched the water washing over old footprints in the sand, erasing them. I walked in the edge of the surf, mindless that the hems of my pant legs were getting wet, and let my thoughts fly out over the waves.

*　*　*

Spring break, 1985. Caroline and I had the house all to ourselves for the first time. My parents had decided that they didn't want to spend a week in chilly April at a nearly deserted Smith, so they hadn't demurred when I suggested Caroline and I go alone. We were so excited about the prospect that we exceeded all speed limits along the back highways from Chapel Hill to Southport.

We opened the house up and stood on the front deck in each other's arms, kissing passionately for all to see. Of course, there was no one to see us. One of the handlers at the ferry had told us there were only about fifty people on the island, and most were staying in the Villas or further up the beach where the most rental property was.

"A whole week of paradise," Caroline sighed, leaning over the rail. "I intend to make love to you until you aren't capable of intelligent speech."

"Darling, you do that to me every time."

She smiled and winked. "I've got something special planned for this trip."

"And I thought I was going to get some studying done."

Caroline laughed at my pretend dismay and kissed the tip of my nose lovingly. I reached for her, but she evaded my grasp and dashed back inside. I gave hot pursuit, capturing her finally in the master bedroom. We fell across the king sized bed, our lips meeting in a sudden frenzy.

I made love to her, in the way she liked best, sitting back on my heels with her resting on my thighs and her legs wrapped around my waist, my hand cupped to her, thrusting fully as she lifted herself against me, my mouth hungry on her breasts. Her hair fell across me, a dark canopy over my wicked lips and tongue, teeth scraping her nipples, teasing and taking until she at last surrendered herself to me in a long wailing, a spasm of heat and wetness.

When she had finished, I simply rose onto my knees and continued forward until I was on top of her, pressing her into the mattress, my fingers never leaving her tightness. I moved against her again with my hips, joining her the second time in orgasm, my mouth cutting off her scream of pleasure.

We fell asleep still tangled in each other's arms.

*   *   *

I shook myself from the memory and cursed the wetness between my thighs with a vehemence born of frustration. The last thing I needed was to spend an entire summer reliving scenes from a time so far gone that it hardly seemed like my life. The beach was rapidly emptying, as the incoming tide combined with the lengthening shadows to drive people back to their houses. I noticed a foursome of women walking toward me, chatting among themselves. I half-wished I could feel that comfortable, but I've always felt like a loner on Smith. Something about it just makes me so introspective I can't imagine being there with a group.

And then there's Caroline. Always Caroline.

The women and I passed each other, and I noted that three of them were in my mother's age group. One looked vaguely familiar, but I couldn't place where I had seen her before. The fourth woman, lagging a bit behind, was probably daughter to one of the others.

She was tall, and her sandy-blonde hair fell loose down her back. She was heavy set, but muscular, and fit in the cotton shorts and polo shirt she wore quite well. I glanced at her face as she passed, and was struck with a sense of familiarity. It was a handsome face, not exactly pretty but striking.

We passed without comment but after I had gone a few more yards I had to look back. My eyes met with the young woman's; she had been watching me pass as well. There was a moment when I actually stopped walking, then she turned back around and continued after the others, taking long strides to close the distance between herself and her companions. I turned back shortly thereafter, and caught sight of them off down the beach climbing the stairs of one of the public accesses.

I thought I saw the girl looking my way again, then they were gone from view. I glanced at my watch and sped up a little. Melissa would have dinner ready and I didn't want to keep her waiting.

II.

Seven o'clock rolled around too soon for me, and I finished styling my hair with a sort of hopelessness that I thought I had outgrown. I consider myself to be a mature, adult woman, yet something about Smith Island made me feel like I was tagging along after mother and daddy again.

Except that mother and daddy were dead and I was the heiress. Melissa was waiting for me in the den, her drink thoughtfully hidden in a plastic tumbler. She was psychic sometimes, I swear.

"Ready to roll, oh great one?"

"I suppose. I'll warn you, don't suggest that you're unattached or they'll be all over you."

Melissa smiled and winked. "OK. I'll tell them I'm with you."

I refrained from smacking her across the rump. "Let's go, comic genius." I drove.

We could just as easily have walked, it was less than a half-mile, but I didn't feel the urge to go wandering around with the sun getting ready to set. One problem with the beach – mosquitoes. We pulled up at the villa – really more of a freestanding condo – behind about ten other carts and headed up to the inquisition.

Janie Millikan met us at the door with her usual smile.

"I'm so glad you stopped by! Come on in. Roger – fix these two something to drink."

Melissa had a beer and I spent about five minutes convincing my dad's old golfing buddy that I really only wanted a soda. Southerners of my parents era are strange about alcohol somehow. They feel like they're being poor hosts if they can't get you to drink. In fact, Roger Millikan had fixed me the strongest 'weak' Bloody Mary I've ever tasted, when I was only nineteen.

I caught a glimpse of Melissa across the room, being introduced to a couple I didn't know, then Janie was by my arm propelling me over to the fireplace where a man about my age stood chatting with Jane Eder. I suppose he was attractive, if sandy blonde hair that was already thinning and that inescapable golf tan everyone in the south seems to have count as attractive on a man. "Katie, I'd like you to meet someone. This is Doctor John Inabinet. John, this is Katie Jenkins, Bob Jenkins' daughter. John's a plastic surgeon. Of course, you know Jane."

"Mrs. Eder. Nice to meet you Doctor Inabinet."

"John, please. Your old man and I played many a round down here. So sorry about Bob. I warned him about his cholesterol. I've heard a lot about you."

I doubted he'd heard it all, or he wouldn't have been so polite. I found myself wishing I had stayed home as he began to drone on; same old stuff, where he went to school, who he knew, what his handicap was. I really never could understand how a man's handicap could have anything to do with his worth as a person, unless of course he was on the pro tour. I caught my attention wandering as he began to discuss how his practice was going. I was beginning to think about asking Roger for one of his weak drinks when someone came up behind me.

"Hi! God, imagine seeing you here!" I turned and found myself staring at the woman from the beach. She raised an eyebrow at me and moved her eyes over my shoulder toward John.

"Uh, hi! John, excuse me for a moment, will you?"

The woman took my arm and led me out onto the deck. "You looked like you were suffering."

I laughed at her comment. "Was it that obvious?"

She shrugged and stuck out her hand. I took it. "Jennifer Brooks. You're Katherine Jenkins, right?"

"Yes! How did you – Jennifer Brooks? Jenny Brooks? Lynne's little sister?" She smiled and nodded. "God, the last time I saw you, you were just a little scrawny thirteen year old! You grew up."

"And out. I guess the family weight curse caught up with me. It's been what – fourteen years?" I agreed. "Did you hear about Lynne and Steven Peters?"

"Three summers ago – yes, someone mentioned it. How are they?" Lynne was one of my dear friends during high school, but college sent us drifting in two totally different directions. She had married another of our classmates and they were recreating the perfect southern couple vignette while I struggled to survive the West Coast lesbian scene with my sanity intact.

"Oh, pretty well I guess. They're expecting their first this November."

"Well, tell them I sent love." Somehow, having such a normal conversation with her seemed very out of place. I couldn't believe how nicely that little teenaged terror had grown up. I remembered her as the kid who waited until we were just comfortable on the beach before pouring sand all over our oiled bodies. I recalled that she always did have long legs - she could outrun me even then, and I was almost twenty one.

"So, are you as bored as I am?"

I shook myself and refocused on the present. Jenny was looking at me in an odd sort of way. "Yeah, I guess I am. I should go rescue Mel before Janie Millikan sets John on her."

"Your friend? Well, grab her and let's blow this popsicle stand." I nodded and went back inside.

As I had suspected, Janie was in the process of introducing Melissa to the good doctor just as I came up. I nudged Melissa and smiled disarmingly at John.

"I'm sorry, Janie, John. But we really have to run. It was a long trip, and I'm just awfully worn out." Melissa threw me a silent thank you with her eyes.

"Well, it was so nice of you girls to stop by. I expect to see more of you while you're here." I agreed that we would, knowing that anything else would be impossible, and guided Melissa back out to the porch where Jenny was lounging against the rail staring across the lagoon toward the golf course.

"Melissa, this is Jenny Brooks. She's Lynne Peters' little sister. Jenny, this is my room mate, Mel Frankel." Mel shook hands with the athletic younger woman.

"A pleasure," Jenny said, her smile showing even white teeth. "Any friend of Katie's is like family to me."

I glanced over at her when she made that rather strange remark, but she wasn't paying me any attention, and Melissa didn't seem to notice it. I indicated the stairs leading down from the deck to the street.

"I think we ought to leave before Janie gets suspicious. Did you have something in mind, Jenny?" Jenny started down the steps before answering.

"Anything is better than this. I was going to take a walk along the beach. Care to join me?"

"Not me," Melissa averred. "I'm wiped out. You go, Katherine. Might as well start laying those ghosts to rest right away." I swiveled on my toes and glared at her, but Jenny was the one who responded.

"We've all got ghosts here," she said absently. "That's why we can't ever leave for good." I heaved a sigh. I would enjoy a walk, and I wanted to hear what Jenny had been up to.

"Is it all right if I drop you off, Melissa?" She nodded and climbed onto the cart. "Did you bring a cart, Jenny, or would you like to ride with me?"

"Mom's here, so I'd better ride with you." She stepped gracefully into the front seat, next to Melissa.

I got in on the driver's side. It was very close with three of us in the front seat, but I noticed Melissa was smiling and knew I would here all sorts of comments when I got back. One thing about Melissa that has always irritated me; she can make a lewd remark about anything, no matter how mundane.

We chatted conversationally on the way back to the house, and when we piled out of the cart, Melissa winked at me. "I'll just go on up now."

"Yeah, you just do that," I growled, feigning a boot to her rear end. She laughed and trotted up the stairs, leaving Jenny and me alone by the garage. "I'll park the cart .... "

"Take your time. You know, your place really brings home how much the beach has eroded in the last fifteen years."

"Yeah. Uh, would you like a drink to take with you?" I felt a little nervous now that it was just the two of us. The last time I had seen Jenny was the last summer Caroline and I had spent here, the summer Caroline died.

"Sure. Can you whip up a vodka Collins?" I gestured to the stairs, and she preceded me up them.

"We just got in, so things are a little disorganized," I apologized as I stepped to the bar. She came up close to me and leaned against the counter right next to where I was working. Her forearm brushed against mine and I was aware of a sudden prickling of heat dashing up my arm and through my chest.

"Only one glass?" She cocked her head and looked at me when I offered her the drink.

"I don't drink socially." Her laugh was hearty, almost too loud for a woman her size. Almost.

"Good God! I remember you and Lynne putting away cases at a time. What happened to that devil-may-care teenager?" I felt the heat rushing to my face. I had no need to explain myself to her.

"I grew up." When Jenny saw the look on my face, she suddenly sobered.

"I'm sorry. I – do you want me not to take this? I mean, if it will bother you or anything ...."

I forced myself to relax. "No, it doesn't bother me. I'm not a recovering alcoholic or anything like that."

"Oh. Okay. Well, grab a Co'cola or something and let's go." I got a soda and we went down to the beach via the front stairs.

* * *

The light was fading as the sun vanished over the mainland, a deep velvet darkness creeping across the sea like an approaching storm. The sand underneath my tennis shoes was littered with debris from the receding tide, and the waves broke more calmly in the ebbing flow. We struck out at once toward East Beach, away from the river. Jenny walked with easy strides, and I had to stretch my legs to match her. She was perhaps five inches taller than my 5'7", and she still carried herself with the carefree air of a girl, while I had bent to a studious life of business suits and pumps.

We went in silence for a little while, communing with the evening and the sounds of nature that came to us on the breeze. Then, all at once, Jenny stopped and turned to me.

"Do you still miss Carrie Dunn?" I turned white and stared at her blankly for a long moment. "I was just wondering if that was one of the ghosts your friend wanted you to bury."

"I don't like to talk about Caroline." I didn't know what else to say. Jenny had been too young to realize that Caroline and I were lovers; she couldn't possibly know that I was a lesbian. Why was she asking me such a question?

"I'm sorry again. I seem to have a bad case of foot in mouth disease tonight. I'm not usually this stupid." She took a long drink and stared past me across the water. I had the distinct impression that she wanted to say more, and didn't dare.

"It's all right. It was a long time ago, and yes, I'm fairly well over it."

Jenny sighed. "Well, I pretty much ruined the mood, didn't I? Do you want to head back?"

"No. Let's keep going for a little while. Tell me what you've been up to. Did you go to Duke like you said you were going to?"

"No," she laughed, relaxing. "When it came time to decide I went for Randolph-Macon. Me, at a women's college. I never thought that would happen. But they offered me a partial lacrosse scholarship, so I took it. Turned out to be more enjoyable than I had expected. I majored in art."

"Do you teach, then?" She looked at me and grinned, shaking her head.

"No way. I have a gallery in Raleigh. Dad fronted me the money to get it going so long as I didn't take post-grad at Duke. You know how he is about the Blue Devils. So I got my Masters at Carolina. Are you a Ph.D. yet?"

"Uh, no. I dropped out when my father died. I've been managing his portfolio since then. I guess I've become a professional investor." She made a face.

"Sounds dry to me." I shrugged. "Married?"

"No. You?"

"Nope. Still a virgin, technically." I coughed and glanced over to see if she was joking. Her face was flat, though she had raised an eyebrow at my reaction. "Hey, there's a few of us left. I got smart early."

"I suppose so." Technically, I supposed I could consider myself a virgin, since the only man I had ever slept with had been Frasier Cunningham, when we were both sixteen. It hadn't been a very pleasant experience.

"You're what, thirty-five now?"

"Thirty-four," I responded stiffly, not wanting to be reminded of that upcoming milestone in my life. Jenny lapsed into silence.

The moon came up over the horizon, a thin slice of silver against the dark sky. Above us, the Milky Way was breaking through the last of the day, glittering fiercely. We walked along, kicking at shells, until a glance at my watch told me it was almost nine. I mentioned it to Jenny, and we turned back toward my house.

*   *   *

On the way back, Jenny walked closer to me, closely enough that I could catch the scent of coconut oil on her skin. Probably sunscreen, I decided, and ignored the thrill of pleasure I felt. I could sense her muscular frame next to me, and glanced up to study her face, illuminated by the crescent of the moon.

Her lips were sensual in the half-light, curled into a private smile. Her nose was short and tipped up on the end, but it seemed appropriate to her round, open face. She still had the same scattering of freckles that I remembered from so long ago. Her bangs fell across her forehead in reckless abandon, though she kept brushing them out of her way with her left hand.

Her neck was muscled and short, her shoulders broad for a woman, her upper arms thick in the polo shirt she wore. My gaze traveled down the three buttons of the shirt to the curve of her ample bosom; there I caught myself, sweating, and pulled my attention rapidly to the ocean. There was an ache in my stomach that I had not felt for a long time, a long slow burn radiating into my chest and down my legs.

"Katie?" I realized she had been talking to me, and looked back over into her green eyes. They seemed to glow in the moonlight.

"I'm sorry, did you say something?"

"Yes, I did. You're about a million miles away all of a sudden. I was wondering if you and Melissa would like to play doubles tomorrow with Tracy Andrews and me."

"Oh, I guess so. What time?" She shrugged.

"I'll have to call you. Around ten, depending on what court time I can get." We continued the rest of the way back to the house in companionable silence, while I considered the reactions my body was having to hers.

I have not been without sex for longer than six months in my adult life. But never had I felt this sudden ache, this unadulterated desire, spring so violently and unexpectedly from my belly. I couldn't explain how Jenny could affect me that way. She was a profoundly striking woman, yes. But nothing in her attitude or appearance gave me any reason to believe she might be a lesbian.

Maybe it's the walk, I told myself. I hadn't been on a moonlit walk along a beach with someone since Caroline. Jenny wasn't a total stranger to me, even though it had been more than half her life since I had last seen her; that familiarity could have contributed to my feeling of want. Or it could have been the lovemaking I had remembered earlier.

But I couldn't deny that I wanted her; the woman next to me, the woman that Jenny Brooks had become. I wanted to put my arms around her and press my body against hers, pull her to the soft sand above the storm line, kiss her face, her lips, her throat....

Get a grip on yourself, Katherine, I admonished myself firmly. I was just reacting to old memories, to the romanticism that the island air had always stirred in me. In the morning, when I wasn't so tired, and I had started to grow accustomed to the steady rhythm of the surf and the brackish smell of the air, I would look at her and see Jenny Brooks, my high school chum's little sister, the one who used to torment us so mercilessly.

"We're here, Katie," Jenny's voice broke into my thoughts. I shook myself and looked at her, then at the house.

"I'll drive you home," I said, sounding almost mechanical. Jenny gave me an odd little sideways glance, then nodded. I drove her to her parents' summer house, a large Cape Cod affair suitable for year 'round living. It was one of the original houses on the island, and I had grown up envious of the Brooks for owning it.

Dr. and Mrs. Brooks actually resided in Winston-Salem. Lynne and Jennifer had been pampered children, driven into Greensboro daily by a maid to attend the Guilford County Day School, the private schools in Winston-Salem having been deemed academically insufficient by the overbearing Mrs. Brooks. I had never been comfortable around that woman.

I stopped the cart in front of the house and waited for Jenny to climb out. She paused just as she started to, and turned to me, giving me a totally unexpected hug.

"I'm so glad to see you again, Katie," she said. "I hope we can be great friends this summer."

"Yes, great ... friends." If she detected the hesitation in my voice, she didn't say anything, just got out and waved as she trotted up to the front door. I sighed and drove off toward my own humble house.

When she touched me, I had felt the ball of heat in my stomach pulsate outward like a supernova, engulfing me with a tingling, hungry feeling, the very cells of my body crying out for a satisfaction that only she could give. That sensation was slow to fade, and my hands were still trembling when I got back to the house.

I plugged in the cart and mounted the stairs slowly, fighting to keep myself under control. Melissa met me at the doorway, with a tumbler in her hand which she pressed on me immediately.

"Take, drink, this is the best thing for you right now." I drank, and tasted rum under the Coke Cola.

"You know how I feel about –"

"You need it," she repeated, cutting me off. "I can see how off-balance you are. You've been strange since we got off that damn dinghy."

"It was a fairly large passenger ferry, Melissa."

"There are times when even you can benefit from the calming properties of a drink." I sighed and agreed with her. The alcohol tasted good going down. "So, what's the scoop on young Miss Brooks?"

"She invited us to tennis tomorrow. Ten-ish. I agreed for us."

"Fine. But what else? Is everyone in her family so divinely handsome?" I sighed. When Melissa smelled a story, she wouldn't stop until she got what she wanted. So I related my memories of Jenny as a thirteen year-old terror. I didn't dare tell her how my belly had been reacting all evening. When I had finished, she sat back and frowned lightly. "So she was on the island when Caroline died?"

"Yes, she was. But she was thirteen."

"Oh." It was an 'Oh' that meant Melissa had made some deep psychological assessment, and that she wasn't going to share. I took another drink.

"Go to bed. I'm going to stay up for a while and work." Melissa shrugged and got up. I watched her walk back to her bedroom, then went to the counter and turned on my computer.

Ten minutes later I knew that working was no good. With a long sigh, I shut things down and went upstairs to my room. I was in the loft because Caroline and I had slept in both the downstairs bedrooms and I couldn't bear to look at either of those beds again.

I unlatched the sliding door that led from the loft onto the upper balcony, and stepped out into the breeze. Leaning against the rail, I looked down over the oily blackness of the ocean and the dim shimmering of the sand. It was all so peaceful and serene. Like eternity.

Then I saw a figure walking toward the water, a lithe woman, with flowing black hair and white skin, nude. She turned and beckoned to me, then waded out into the water.

I stared. There was no mistaking her, not from this distance.

It was Caroline.

III.

I could feel my heart pounding against my chest, my breath catching in my throat as it closed up. I strained forward against the night, trying to discern her body among the waves. She turned to face me once more, and I could see her mouth moving as if to speak, then she turned and dove through a breaking wave, and vanished.

Feeling nauseous, I threw myself back into the house, taking the stairs down from the loft two at a time. I heard Melissa behind me, coming from her room as I pulled open the door and dashed out onto the deck.

I half-fell down the outside steps, and stumbled across the sand to where I had seen Caroline. I looked wildly around, at the water, the sand, for some physical sign of her. There were no footprints leading into the water, no body breaking the surface of the ocean.

Melissa came up beside me, putting her hand on my arm. "Katherine? What happened?"

"I – I saw her." The words sounded idiotic to my ears, but I plunged on. "I saw Caroline."

Melissa's arms went around my waist, turning me away from the water. She pushed my head down onto her shoulder and held it there. "Oh, baby. I was afraid this would happen."

I didn't want to be comforted. I had seen someone, I knew I had. But Melissa is stronger than I am, and she wouldn't let me go. I gave up trying.

"I'm all right now, Melissa." I said finally, then straightened up and looked at her. Melissa has this habit of putting her arms around people. Usually I find the affection comforting, but now it only made me feel awkward.

"Come back inside, Katherine. Tell me what happened." As we walked back up to the house, I explained what I had seen. Melissa sat me down on the couch and offered me a cup of tea, which I accepted. When she had brought two steaming cups, she sat next to me and put a hand on my knee. "I've known you for almost ten years, Kate. That's a long time. I know you're usually very level-headed."

"I know, Melissa. But I saw someone."

"I'm not saying you didn't. But it wasn't Caroline. She's dead, Katherine. She's been dead for a long, long time. And I don't believe you saw a ghost."

"Caroline used to love to swim nude." I was being stubborn, and I knew it. It had just seemed so real to me. Melissa sighed.

"You're tired, Katherine. You've been working yourself far too hard the past six months. Go to bed, take your sleeping pill, and sleep. You'll feel better in the morning, I swear." I looked over at her, her short, curly blonde hair and blue eyes and angelic face belying the keen intelligence and hard will that lay beneath.

"Okay, Melissa. You're right. I've just been overwrought tonight, that's all. It's so strange coming back after so long ...." She nodded and hugged me.

"Bed."

"Yes, ma'am."

I went into the bathroom to brush my teeth and change. I kicked my shoes off into the corner, then pulled off my pants and shirt and dropped them on top of the shoes. Reaching back, I unfastened my bra and took it off, hooking it over the doorknob. Melissa was constantly complaining about this habit of mine, but I had learned early in my college years that it was easier to find it the next morning when I left it somewhere obvious.

As I ran my toothbrush around my teeth, I found myself comparing my short, spiked auburn hair and dark brown eyes with Jenny's hair and eyes, my long oval face, too light for someone who used to spend every possible moment out-of-doors, with her deep tan and inviting smile. I wondered what Jenny thought of me; I thought I looked like an old photograph of the girl I had been at twenty; a washed-out, faded, wrinkled photograph.

With a sigh, I reached for my nightshirt, pausing to look at my naked body in the mirror. At least that part of me was still in good shape. Melissa dragged me to the spa regularly, where I could at least read Investor's Business Daily and The Wall Street Journal while pedaling the LifeCycle or walking on the treadmill.

I turned sideways and glanced over my hip at the small tattoo on my left buttock, a pink triangle with intersecting black and white female symbols superimposed over it. The tattoo was the result of one of my nights of drunken self-pity, when a girl I had been dating for only a week suggested we get ourselves tattooed to show our support for 'wimmin everywhere'. Things like that are why I don't drink much any more.

I pulled on the nightshirt and turned out the light on my way upstairs. I closed the sliding door, hoping that less than half of the mosquitoes in a five-acre radius had decided to come inside, and pulled back the sheets to my bed. Crawling in, I felt the coolness of the cotton against my bare legs and arms, shifted into the pillow, and let myself relax.

*   *   *

We met Jenny and Tracy at the Club at ten the next morning. It was already hot, and unlike the previous day, there was no breeze to stir the humidity around and make it bearable. Melissa looked uncomfortable in her tennis whites, sweat already trickling down from curls plastered against her forehead. She has the disadvantage of being large framed and stocky, and I didn't doubt that she would be soaked by the end of the game.

I didn't know Tracy Andrews, so introductions were made and we began our game. It was a good match, the four of us being of equal ability. We decided to alternate partners instead of playing straight sets, and when it came my turn to play with Jenny, I moved to her side of the net expecting no response from my body. I was sure I had gotten over the initial attraction.

I was wrong.

The moment I stepped up to her, I smelled her musk over the scent of Polo cologne. The only women I knew who wore Polo were lesbians. It is also the only cologne in the world that makes me weak in the knees. Jenny's shirt was sticking to her, the outline of her sports bra clearly visible as the only part of her shirt not soaked through.

Her nipples were hard.

I felt a rush of moisture that was not the least bit related to the temperature or to tennis. At the same time, her eyes met mine and I saw a smile start deep within them, a smile that set off the same supernova in my stomach as her hug had the night before.

"Shall I serve?" Her voice was low, husky, sensual. It sent a shiver down my spine. Not trusting myself to answer, I nodded and hurried to the net. Several men came onto the court next to us and began to hit up.

I heard her grunt, and the ball whizzed past me into Tracy's court. She returned it deep and Jenny lobbed it toward Melissa. Melissa hit it to me and I buried it in the net. It was the first net ball I had hit all day. I bent to retrieve it, and turned to toss it back to Jenny, only to find her walking toward me, hand outstretched.

As I handed the ball to her, she grinned at me and winked. "Pay attention to the game, not the scenery."

I blushed deeply, and turned back to the net determined to put her out of my mind, glad that she had attributed my lack of focus to the men next to us.

We finished our match and eagerly retired to the grill for lunch and cool drinks. Over chilled lobster salad and iced tea, we chatted about island gossip, tennis, and the changes I had noticed to the island since my last visit.

Tracy excused herself first, saying that she had to meet her husband for a round of golf and wanted a shower first, and then Melissa asked if she could take the cart and go back to the house, saying she wanted to go swimming. I shrugged and handed her the keys. She smiled at me and put a hand on my shoulder before leaving.

Jenny studied her ice cubes for a long silent moment, then lifted her gaze to my face. I melted into her eyes, and found myself wanting to reach out and take her hand. *Whoa, Katherine, get hold of yourself!* I forced a pleasant smile and dug at the remains of my salad.

"So, how do you like it in Seattle?" Jenny's tone was light. She ran her forefinger around the rim of her glass.

"I love it. It's far more – satisfying than living in North Carolina." I poked at the mint leaves in my glass with my ice tea spoon. "How do you like Raleigh?"

"Not much night life. Not the sort I like, anyway." Her voice had dropped back into that sensual half-whisper. I crossed my legs and clenched them together against the ache in my groin. I couldn't understand what was happening to me. "Are you all right, Katie?"

"Yes," I managed to say in a normal tone. "I'm just not used to the heat yet." She smiled at me with the most seductive smile I have ever seen on a woman's face, a smile which, had I seen it on any woman that I knew to be a lesbian, would have resulted in my taking her home. A smile which I would ever after call simply The Smile.

"Oh, but Katherine, it hasn't even started to get hot yet."

*   *   *

I found Melissa laying on a towel on the beach. She was on her stomach, her arms by her sides, her eyes closed. I considered fishing an ice cube out of my tea and dropping it on her back, but she sensed my presence before I could act and rolled over.

"Hi. Did you and Jenny have a nice chat?"

"Yes." I had decided, watching Jenny at the club joking with the busboy and the waiter, that she was quite plainly and simply a natural tease. She seemed to just ooze sensuality, and I had that afternoon seen the effect she had on men.

"Ready for a swim?" Melissa climbed to her feet and adjusted her bathing suit. I had my suit on, but glanced dubiously at the ocean.

"I think I'll just watch for now. You go on ahead." Melissa shrugged and started down the beach toward the water.

I settled myself into the lounge chair beside Melissa's towel, and looked through my Vuarnet's along the shore. There were several groups of bathers in the surf, and other clusters and singles wandered up and down the sand.

Dropping my head back, I closed my eyes and let the sun beat down on my face and shoulders. My mind was filled again with the image of Jenny Brooks smiling at me across the table at the grill. I felt my body reacting, wondered at the obsession I seemed to be developing for the woman.

I had to do something about it; I had been on the island less than twenty-four hours, and I already had the worst case of the hots in the history of the world. If I didn't get myself under control, it promised to be a long, excruciating summer.

I resolved to call and ask Angela Millikan to play golf as soon as I got back inside. I also told myself that I would spend more time working on my computer; the market was acting overly volatile and I didn't need to let my attention slide.

And there were plenty of things for Melissa and me to do. We could rent a canoe and explore the marshes of the island, which would give us ample chance to photograph much of the varied wildlife of the area. Melissa was a camera fanatic, and had already expressed an interest in the trip.

We could volunteer at the Conservancy for turtle watch. I remembered as a child sitting on the beach with my parents and others, waiting with flashlights and bated breath for the loggerhead turtles to pull themselves out of the dark sea to dig their nests and lay their eggs. When the Smith Island Foundation was created to manage the construction explosion, the Conservancy took over the turtle watch, though residents were still encouraged to volunteer.

We could take the ferry back across to Southport and drive up to Wilmington in a rented car, for shopping and dinner. I wasn't sure Melissa would want to make the crossing any more times than necessary, but I thought I could probably convince her to go with me if shopping was involved.

Of course, there was always tennis, croquet, horseback riding, sunbathing, shell hunting, swimming, dining at the club or the restaurant at the marina, reading, and just exploring the natural beauty of the island.

I, myself, enjoyed just driving along the narrow streets exploring the mysterious atmosphere. It was said that Blackbeard the pirate had used Smith as a base of operations, that somewhere in the marshes, buried under years of shifting sand and water, was his treasure. There was a long history to the island, a history full of pirates and Indians, lighthouses and shipwrecks.

As a teenager, I had wanted to find Blackbeard's treasure. I spent long hours tromping around the backwoods looking for clues to where his hideout had been. Sometimes, Lynne Brooks would go with me, sometimes Caroline. That was before we had become lovers.

I discovered that I was a lesbian when I was seventeen. Caroline was my first, and our relationship lasted almost four years, growing stronger with each passing month despite the need for secrecy and subterfuge. We had both chosen to attend the University of North Carolina at Chapel Hill, in order to be together.

That was a bit of subtle maneuvering on our part. Since there is such a great demand for dorm rooms at UNC-CH, most of the time freshmen have to live off campus. We were able to convince our parents that we should share an apartment, and that we were willing to make do with a one bedroom to save money. We had twin beds in that one bedroom, and I don't recall ever sleeping in mine.

I glanced down at my watch and was pleased to see that I had been sitting there for almost half an hour without thinking about Jenny. I started to close my eyes again when I felt speckles of water splattering me. I looked up at Melissa who shook her head at me again, sending more water droplets flying.

"I can't believe you're still just sitting there. The water's great!"

"I was just relaxing. You know, the act of doing nothing?" She grinned at me.

"Well, if you're going to do nothing then I'm going to finish my sunbathing." She flopped down across her towel and rolled onto her back, reaching for her sunglasses. I watched her for a moment, then closed my eyes again and let the sun's warm rays lull me back into my contemplative mood.

*   *   *

I played golf with Angela the next day, had lunch with her and Janie at the villa, then went on an abbreviated round of social visits. I knew I had to stop by and say hello to the Brooks', and I half hoped Jenny wouldn't be there. I decided to put that off until the next day and returned to the house to check the market.

The next few days passed in a blur as I slowly immersed myself back into the rhythm of life on the island. I was a Seattle workaholic, and it took me a while to remember that things just weren't rushed at Smith. I had to forcibly slow myself down, to not get bored. I played tennis with Jenny, Angela and Tracy one day, golf with John Inabinet the next, accepted invitations to lunches and dinners, social hours and so forth.

Jenny seemed to be ignoring me, which was fine. She came by maybe once a day, but there wasn't any teasing in her voice like there had been those first two days, she didn't touch me or make the sorts of comments that had so flustered me. She and I did things together, and I found that she was a very nice person to talk to. I was even beginning to think of her as a friend. I thought that perhaps her new constraint toward me would give me a chance to get my libido under control. In reality, all it did was intensify my longing; when she wasn't around, I wanted her to be. She not only had me in a sexual frenzy, she had me in an intellectual one too.

My dream about Caroline came back. I have had this same dream on and off ever since she drowned. I can see her lying on the beach, her long dark hair streaming out around her limply, as I try desperately to pump air back into her lungs. Invariably, I wake up shivering, wanting to cry and not able to.

I didn't mention the dream to Melissa, but I think she could tell. About a week after our arrival, I was sitting on the deck staring over my coffee at the ocean when she came out of the house behind me. I knew she was there, but she didn't speak and I didn't turn around. After a few moments, she sighed heavily.

"If I had known this trip was going to turn you into such a zombie, I would have recommended against it."

"You aren't my therapist," I returned, glancing back at her. "I would have come alone if I had to."

"You're dreaming again, aren't you." I nodded and took a sip of coffee. It was still too hot; it burned my tongue and the roof of my mouth. Silently, I cursed. "What have you got planned today? I'm going to play croquet with the Pattersons."

"I'm playing golf with Jenny."

"Well, have fun. I don't see why anyone would want to spend all that time whacking a little white ball with a stick. You just have to walk after it and whack it again." I smiled softly and turned around to face her.

"It's Zen, Melissa. If I can get through a round of golf without wanting to chuck my clubs in the nearest lake, then I know I've achieved inner peace."

She laughed and leaned against the wall of the house. "You're silly sometimes."

I shrugged. "I know."

"Well, I'll make breakfast if you do dishes." I joined her at the door.

"Deal."

*   *   *

Jenny teed up on the first hole and took her practice swing. I watched her powerful follow through and wondered idly if she lifted weights to build such a strong physique. She constantly complained about her weight, but though I had yet to see her in a bathing suit, I could see nothing but muscle in her arms and legs. She wore a short sleeved striped rugby shirt and a pair of light pink Bermuda shorts.

She addressed the ball and took a mighty whack at it. It shot through the air and landed almost to the green, a good one hundred eighty yards. I left my drive about twenty yards shorter, and we got in the cart and started down the fairway.

"You seem a little preoccupied today, Katie," Jenny commented as she drove. I glanced over at her.

"I didn't sleep well." She gave me a strange grin and lapsed into silence. My fairway shot landed at the edge of the green and rolled toward the pin, leaving me a long birdie putt. Hers landed no more than five yards from the pin. She walked up while I pulled the cart around, then I two-putted for par and she sank hers for a birdie.

"Will you be playing in the Ladies Tournament next month?" I asked her after watching her power another long drive down the second hole fairway. We were playing from the white tees instead of the red, to make it more challenging. She waited until after I had shanked my drive, which hit a fortunately placed palmetto tree and ricocheted back into the fairway, to answer.

"Probably. Are you?"

"I doubt it. I'm not a very good player."

"You underestimate your abilities," she observed. Not sure how to answer, I shrugged and started back to the cart. She followed me slowly.

"I don't have a lot of time to practice at home. It takes more time than I had thought it would to track the market. It's a full time job."

"So how are you managing here?" I blushed softly.

"I brought my computer. It has a modem so I can download closing prices. And I got a mailbox and transferred my subscriptions for the summer." She laughed.

"On vacation? Sounds like you've just opened a branch office." I was silent. I didn't want to try and explain how much it meant to me that I was responsible for so much money. My father had left me a fairly wealthy woman, and I intended to keep myself that way. We finished up the hole without comment, then went across the road to the third tee.

"Nice drive," she commented when I hit a long ball down the middle of the fairway. She put hers just in front of the lake on the left, startling an alligator that had been sunning there. He slid noiselessly into the water and disappeared.

"You know, I never asked what your gallery specializes in," I said a few minutes later, having hit a 3-iron almost to the green of the par 5. She leaned back in the seat and laughed.

"Women's art. I have some of my work there, but mostly other women. Paintings, ceramics, sculpture, stained glass, a little of everything."

"What do you do?"

"Jewelry. I like working in stained glass, especially earrings. You know, you'd look nice in a pair I'm working on now. Your hair is just the right length and color. I also work in cloisonné. I was trained in sculpture, but I didn't have the patience to wait for the work to progress, so I found something smaller and more instantly gratifying."

"That sounds interesting. How's business?" She shot me a look that made me think I was treading on thin ice with that question, and changed the subject.

"How long have you and Melissa lived together?" I thought for a moment.

"About seven years. I've got a house just outside of Seattle, in Ballard." Her face went blank for a split second, then she was smiling again.

"Must be nice and settled."

"I suppose." I thought about my house. It was a big old Victorian, and I had been restoring it since I had first bought it. Things were proceeding much more quickly since my inheritance. While I was gone, it was getting a new roof and a remodeled kitchen. A lesbian contractor I knew was doing the work.

The upstairs had originally had five bedrooms, but I had converted a small back room into a master bath. Melissa's room was on the opposite side of the hall, with its own small balcony.

My room had a glass sunroom to one side, though the view wasn't much. I had it set up as a breakfast room.

Melissa and I lived together, but we didn't see a lot of each other in the big house. She had converted the back bedroom downstairs into an office and saw her clients there, while I spent most of my time in my office upstairs. I supposed it was settled; we shared cooking and cleaning responsibilities, and entertained together. But it wasn't the same as being with someone.

"Your shot," Jenny said, her voice breaking into my thoughts. I glanced at my lie, then selected a chipping wedge and walked over to my ball. I was on a roll; it landed about three feet from the hole and stopped dead. I was virtually guaranteed a birdie.

We finished out the front nine, and Jenny was ahead of me by four strokes. I had lost a ball in the water on six and bogied eight. Jenny seemed a little preoccupied as we went on, and I had a feeling that she should have been more than four strokes up.

We paused at the clubhouse for iced tea and sandwiches, then set out on the back nine. Our conversation was confined to the course conditions and commentary on our shots. Jenny ended up beating me by seven, she scoring a 68 and I a 75. She shook my hand at the clubhouse, and I felt the beginning of an ache, but she dropped my hand so quickly that it didn't have time to fully develop.

"Good round. I guess I should go check in with Mother and see what she wants to do tonight. I heard her mumbling something about bridge."

"Thanks. I'll see you later then?"

"Yeah, I guess." I watched her put her clubs onto her private cart, paying extra attention as she bent over to fasten the strap around the bottom of her bag.

The fabric of her shorts stretched across her hips and the backs of her thighs, showing how firm and supple they were, and I found myself wondering what she would look like naked, sitting astride my stomach with her hair falling down over her shoulders. She looked up then, caught my frankly appraising gaze, and raised an eyebrow. I blushed and turned away, roughly grabbing my own bag and starting toward my cart.

She didn't come after me, or make a comment as I walked past her, just stood there with her hands on her hips watching me. When I climbed into my cart, she got in hers and drove away.

I put my hands on the steering wheel and rested my head on them. My groin ached with a growing desire; I felt the swelling of my breasts with a hunger almost like pain. I had to do something about this doomed obsession.

IV.

The computer screen filled with figures as I tapped the keys lightly and waited. I highlighted a stock and pulled up the historical data on it then had it printed out. Behind me, one of the local radio stations played The Coasters through the speakers of the stereo.

I punched a few more numbers into my program and idly watched the results. A Coke sat beside me, untouched, and I was listening to the news on CNBC. Melissa had lain down for a nap, leaving me to peruse my stock tables at leisure. The only problem was, my mind was awhirl with other things as well.

I thought about the last summer Caroline and I had spent together, there in that house. I remembered laying on the couch with her against me, the sensation of her lifting my hair and letting fall through her fingers, my hands feeling the warmth of her back and shoulders.

I could recall so much of that summer so easily, despite having tried not to remember for so long. I knew that we had made love under the stars on the deck, that we had run down the beach in the rain, holding hands and collapsing at last on the rug in front of the fireplace, soaked and laughing, only to fall into passion moments later.

I knew that I had cooked her steaks on the grill and she had tried to boil crabs, and that one had climbed up the spoon out of the pot of water and scared her so badly she had dumped the entire pot of scalding water on the floor, burning her legs, and that I had kissed her pain away again and again.

I knew she had liked to climb the stairs of the lighthouse, rickety as they were, that she would kneel over me and tease me until I begged her for release, that she would take me hard and fast before offering herself to me, that she would scream my name over and over when she came under my lips.

I knew what she said to me every night before we went to sleep. She would kiss me and whisper, "We have the rest of our lives to sleep. Let's do something more fun right now." And invariably, we would.

I knew that I loved her more than life itself.

I knew that if we hadn't been half-drunk on champagne in celebration of our upcoming senior year, she wouldn't have drowned in the ocean on that bright August day.

I caught the first sob, but the wall had broken. Tears spilled down my cheeks as I buried my face in my hands and rocked back and forth. I hadn't cried for Caroline in years, and all that time had backed up in me until this moment. Now the floodgates were opened.

Great heaving sobs wracked me, tore my heart into millions of tiny pieces and scattered the pieces across the waves. It was as though it had happened just the day before, so deep and dark was my sorrow, my pain. I couldn't stop myself, couldn't even try. I fought for breath between sobs, feeling the constriction in my throat and the pounding of my lungs.

I felt arms around me, strong, steady. Blindly, I turned into them, allowing myself to collapse against the sturdy chest of the woman who held me. I assumed Melissa had heard me crying and had gotten up. She rocked me gently back and forth, murmuring into my hair. Feeling her against me slowly brought me back to reality, and I was able to start regaining some control of myself. The tears slowed. She kissed my forehead softly, and turned my face into her chest.

"Katherine? Oh, Jenny. What's going on?" I heard Melissa's voice, but it came from the direction of her bedroom, not from beside me. Instantly, the arms released me, and I stumbled to my feet, rubbing the tears from my eyes. Jenny had come to her feet as well, and was looking from me to Melissa with a white face.

"Melissa! I – I thought you weren't here. I .... Oh, Goddess, I'm sorry, Katie. It wasn't what it looked like, I swear, Melissa, I – Goddess, I'm really sorry." She backed toward the door.

Slowly I realized that it had been her arms around me, her chest against my cheek, her lips in my hair .... I felt a churning confusion, a juxtaposition of love for Caroline and desire for Jenny that left me speechless. Melissa took two steps toward me, her face a mask of concern.

Still white, Jenny pushed open the screen door and dashed out. I heard the tires of a golf cart screech as she took off. I stood where I was, still shaking with the aftermath of my tears and the shock of what had happened.

"What the Hell was that all about?" Melissa came to me and gently pushed me back down onto the sofa, sinking down beside me.

"I haven't a clue," I answered slowly. "I was crying, and someone put their arms around me, I thought it was you."

"Why were you crying?" I told her. "I'm sorry, Katherine. But it probably did you good to get it out again. You'll never get over it if you keep hiding your feelings. You keep trying to blame yourself, just when I think you've stopped."

"I can't help but blame myself. I loved her so much. I let her down when she really needed me, and all because I was drunk."

"Katherine, you're only torturing yourself." Melissa put her arm around me and pulled me over against her shoulder. I rested my head on it and sighed. "You'll never have a lasting relationship unless you work through this problem."

"I don't want a relationship, and you know it. I can't put that much of myself on the line again. I'm too old, this time I wouldn't survive it." Knowing that it was futile to argue with me, mainly because we have had this discussion many times in the past, Melissa squeezed me and let go. She got up and went into the kitchen and poured herself an iced tea.

"So I guess we become two old spinsters with about a million cats, eh?" I laughed.

"Yeah, though I have a feeling your butch Belinda may be the one to whisk you off to conjugal bliss." Melissa stuck her tongue out at me.

"Belinda's about as squirrelly as you are. I'm lucky she hasn't taken off on me yet."

"After two years? Not likely. I think you're the one who's afraid of the big C. I've lived through your last two relationships, remember?"

Melissa was headed back into the bedroom. "I don't want to talk about my love life, dearest. I suggest you clean up and see if you can't find Jenny Brooks. I don't know what that was all about, but if you don't get it worked out, you won't be seeing any more of her around her, I guarantee you that."

"What makes you think I care whether she comes around or not?"

From the bedroom, she answered me. "Because if you don't, you're a blind idiot. You like her, and she likes you. Make a friend for a change, okay? I need to have a life, too, sometimes." I threw a small pillow at the door and missed, then sat on the couch and drank my soda, contemplating what she had said about Jenny. I honestly didn't know what to do about her. Part of me wanted to rush out and track her down, and part of me thought it was for the best if she never came back. And since the part of me that wanted to find her was the part between my legs, and I've gotten very good at not listening to that part, I was relatively certain which part would win.

But then, the part between my legs seemed to have joined forces with my stomach and my heart. That made it a more formidable adversary to my mind. I decided to take a drive and try to puzzle out what was going on.

After driving around aimlessly for a while, I decided that as long as I was out, I might as well stop by the chandler's and pick up some of the things we needed at the house, milk, bread, and so forth. I pointed the golf cart in the direction of the marina and lapsed into thought.

As much as I didn't want to, I knew that sooner or later I would have to talk to Jenny about what had happened. I didn't want her to be afraid that I might start spreading rumors about her, and I didn't want her spreading rumors about me. The only question was when to talk to her. I thought that letting some time elapse might me best, to give both of us time to recover.

It felt strange, knowing that all she had done was hold me when I needed someone to hold me, but she had reacted so strangely that I was afraid she might be suspicious about me and Melissa, that she might think I would misinterpret her actions. That's something I hate about being a lesbian; I'm always having to second-guess people's reactions and motivations. It would be so much easier if we could be open about who we were, if we didn't have to hide behind other faces, other lives.

I pulled into the parking lot at the marina and turned off the switch, took the key out of the ignition and got out. I was halfway up the stairs to the chandler's when the door opened and Jenny walked out.

I almost turned around, but then she saw me and I knew I couldn't. I took in a deep breath and went up to her. She stopped as I approached. I could see a blush under her tanned skin. "Hi," I said. "Can we talk?"

She pointed along the walkway toward the marina and we walked over, out of the direct line of entry to the store.

"Look, I'm really sorry ...." She stopped and bit her lip. I smiled gently and shook my head.

"There's no reason. But where did you come from?" She stared at the rough boards of the deck for a moment, and then looked up at me shyly.

"I just wanted to stop by and see if you wanted to go shell-hunting. I saw you crying through the screen, and Melissa didn't seem to be there, and .... I hope she didn't take it the wrong way. You just looked like you needed some comforting."

"I did," I agreed. "Melissa didn't take anything the wrong way. Why should she?" I saw a startled look cross Jenny's face. She looked doubtful for a moment, then puzzled.

"Why should she?" she echoed. "Isn't she your girlfriend?"

"My what?" The words tore from my throat at a roar. Below us, a group of people walking from the ferry landing looked up at us in surprise. I coughed and repeated my words more softly.

Jenny frowned, and took a step backwards. "Your girlfriend. You are still gay, aren't you?"

It was my turn to be startled.

We stared at each other for a long silent moment, then slowly I smiled, then grinned. She smiled back, tentatively.

"You little shit! You knew I was a lesbian when you were thirteen years old?"

"Well, yeah. Christ, anybody within half a mile of that damn lighthouse could hear Carrie Dunn screaming your name out at the top of her lungs. Oh, I'm sorry .... I've said the wrong thing again, haven't I."

The memory pushed at my vision, but I wasn't going to let it get to me again. I had to hear more. "No, go on."

"Lynne didn't know what to do about it. She kept going around muttering 'damn dyke' all the time. I finally told her to stuff a sock in it." I smiled at the thought of proper southern belle Lynne Brooks saying the word dyke.

"So, you assumed that Melissa and I ...." She nodded.

"Yeah. I mean, she is sleeping in the master bedroom. I assumed you were sleeping in there too. And the way you lost your concentration as soon as you got on the other side of the net from her that morning we played tennis, I guessed it was because she was hot and sweaty. Then you said you'd been living together for seven years .... I suppose it sounds stupid now."

"No, not at all." I felt so relaxed all of a sudden. Someone on Smith Island knew I was a lesbian and didn't care. That made me feel wonderful. "We're very good friends, but certainly not lovers. You're brave though, wrapping your arms around a known lesbian while she's in the midst of an emotional crisis. You never know how we might react. I might have kissed you."

I had a feeling the blush started in her toes.

"I doubt that." She started to say more, then glanced over my shoulder and fell silent. I heard footsteps and turned to see Maureen Brooks walking toward us. She carried two canvas bags full of groceries.

"Hello, Mrs. Brooks."

"Hello, Katie. I was wondering when we would run into you. Jennifer, dear, take one of these, would you?" Jenny moved around me and relieved her mother of one of the bags.

"I've been meaning to stop by, but I've been so busy ...." Maureen made a motion of dismissal.

"Oh, it's all right. But you'll have to come to supper one night next week. It's been so long since we've seen you." I nodded dumbly. "I'll be in the cart, Jennifer. Don't be long." She turned around and walked off. I looked back at Jenny and saw the discomfort on her face.

"I suppose you'd best be going," I said.

"Damn, I wish I didn't have to. She's having a bridge party tonight. I hate bridge."

"Well, how would you like to come by my place for dinner tonight? We ordered shrimp yesterday and we were going to boil it up." She smiled.

"Sure! Anything to escape that house. I'll bring the wine."

"Great. How about seven thirty? We can start with cocktails and go from there."

We walked back toward the stairs, talking easily as we had before. I fought with myself, recognizing that I wanted her, and knowing that she knew I was a lesbian didn't make hiding that desire any easier.

As we neared our respective carts, she turned to me and stopped me dead in my tracks. She was giving me The Smile. I felt my knees go weak again, felt a rush of warmth between my legs. I wondered if she knew what that look did to people. Somehow I didn't think so. Otherwise, she wouldn't be giving it with her mother sitting just yards away.

"I can't wait for tonight, Katie."

"Jenny, one thing." If I couldn't ignore The Smile, I could redirect my energy into something else before I lost total control and said something I'd regret. "I don't like to be called Katie."

The Smile deepened, and I felt my heart flip over in my chest. If it were possible to die of pleasure from just a look, I would have done so then. "Then we're even, Katherine. I don't like to be called Jenny."

*　　*　　*

I stretched my bare legs out in front of me and pushed back in the beach chair, feeling little eddies of heat swirling over my sweat-dampened body as I relaxed under the warm sun. Caroline used to call it 'lizarding' when I would sit like this, unmoving, basking in the heat of our local star. I wasn't trying to get a tan; I was just soaking up the rays. I could hear the water rolling in below me, the gentle rhythm like a lullaby.

I slipped into my memories as easily as I could have slipped into the warm Atlantic water. Caroline and I lay side by side, our hands the only part of us touching. I was on my back, she on her stomach. The day was hot, oppressively humid, making any attempt at activity as futile as dowsing in the desert.

"Lover?" Caroline rubbed her fingers across the back of my hand. I made a noise in response. "Where do you think we'll be in fifteen years?"

"Oh, San Francisco, I guess. That's where all the lesbians are, isn't it?" I sensed her movement, opened my eyes despite wanting to keep them closed. She had rolled onto her side and was studying me.

"I mean us, you and me. Do you think we'll still be living together, like we are now?"

"I would hope we'd have a house by then," I replied. She frowned at me, her oval face pulling down into a look that I loved as much as her smile. I loved every expression she had, except the one that she got when she was very angry with me.

"I'm trying to be serious."

"Darling, I can't answer you. There isn't any reason I can think of for us not to spend the rest of our lives together."

"What if we grew apart? You're so studious with your psychology, so clinical sometimes. I'm an artist. Will you be willing to put up with the kind of work schedule I'll have to have?" I turned onto my side and we faced each other. Gently, I caressed her cheek, feeling the soft down.

"You're a very good cellist, C. There won't be any problem with you getting a seat in an orchestra. Or a string quartet. If that fails, you can always become the Joan Baez of the 80's with that guitar style of yours. Even if you never work a single day in your life, I don't care. I love you. I'll be making enough to support us."

"How did I get so lucky to find you?" She put a finger on her lips, then mine. We were always very careful not to kiss in public, lest someone happen along while we were unawares.

"Summer camp is the best place to make friends, mom always says." We laughed.

"What if something happened to you, though?" I stared at her. I didn't like to think about things happening to either of us. We'd been in a car wreck earlier in the spring, and Caroline had gotten a pretty serious concussion.

"Like what?"

"Like, if you were in a wheelchair."

"I could still be a counselor." I looked deeply into her eyes and saw the love in them. "Would you still want me if I was in a wheelchair?"

Caroline nodded emphatically. "Any way I could get you, as long as you were there."

"What if I died?" My mother was very sick with cancer, and I had been thinking a lot about what would happen to my father if she died. I wondered if he would remarry. I wondered what Caroline would do. She considered my question for a long, silent moment.

"I'd go on living, I suppose. I'd have to."

"Would you take another lover?"

"No. Never. You're the only person I'll ever love." I smiled at her, liking the emphatic way she said it.

"I wouldn't either. I've given my heart away, and I don't want it back." Caroline smiled deeply, blushing a little under her tan.

"Not that either of us is going anywhere," she said. "But it does stroke the ego, doesn't it?" I nodded.

"Let's go inside, C. I've got something else that needs a little stroking." She giggled and rolled to her feet. Smiling a silly smile, I followed her toward walkway over the dunes that led to our house.

Melissa's voice interrupted my reverie, calling me from the kitchen, ordering me to get ready for dinner. I sighed, wiped away a couple of tears, and went to shower.

* * *

Melissa sat the ice bucket on the bar at seven fifteen and fixed herself a Bloody Mary. I went into the bathroom, to put the finishing touches on my hair. I had chosen to wear a white silk blouse and black cotton slacks, with a wide red belt. It might have been a little dressy, but I was accustomed to dressing up for dinner.

She wore a long Indian skirt and oversized cotton button-down, with her African necklaces and Birkenstocks. She looked like a beatnik to me when she dressed that way, but I knew she could carry it off. I, on the other hand, would never even attempt it.

"So she knew all along about you," Melissa called from the den. I had just finished explaining our conversation to her as we had fixed the salad in the kitchen.

"Yeah. And she thought we were together." Melissa laughed as I rejoined her. She handed me a glass of ginger ale.

"Sorry, love, you aren't my type."

"I know, I don't have a crew cut, or a motorcycle or the words 'Wimmin Rule' tattooed on my arm." She made a face at me.

"Well, you do have that cute little triangle ...." I slapped at her hand as she went to pinch my bottom. We played like this all the time, it didn't mean anything.

"I'll have to tell Belinda on you," I warned. She held up her hands in mock surrender and took up her drink. "I think I hear someone on the stairs."

A moment later, footsteps sounded on the deck and I saw Jennifer's head pop around the doorframe. "Permission to come aboard?"

"Come on in, Jenny - Jennifer." She pushed open the screen and stepped inside. She was wearing a pair of sharply pressed jeans and a soft blue cotton sweater over a white turtleneck. Her penny loafers looked just shined. In her hand she held two bottles of wine.

"I know you said you don't drink socially, but I thought you might want to use a bottle for the shrimp," she explained as she handed them over. One was a French Chablis, the other a California Dry Riesling Sweet Select, both fairly expensive. I gave them to Melissa, who whistled appreciatively.

"We won't waste those on the shrimp," I said. "Which would you like to open first?" We settled on the Chablis, and I traded my ginger ale for a wine glass.

"You two go on out on the deck while I finish dinner," Melissa ordered, taking her drink with her. I stopped Jennifer when she began to protest.

"She's the gourmet cook. Leave her be or she'll throw a bouquet garnis at you."

"Wise ass," Melissa growled from the kitchen. Jennifer followed me out onto the deck, where a soft breeze was blowing. It would keep the bugs away during dinner. The table was already set, awaiting the food and a match to light the candle in the center.

Jennifer sank down onto the built-in bench along the rail and took a sip of her wine. "Mother was less than thrilled that I was cutting out on her. When do they figure out we're adults?"

"I don't know. I think it has something to do with producing grandchildren." She made a noise and stared down at the deck between her feet.

"Then I'm going to be a kid for a long time."

"No children in your near future?" She looked up at me and shook her head. "Can't say as I blame you. But then I'm a little prejudiced." We drank in silence for a moment.

"Can I ask you a question about Carrie Dunn?" Her face was expressionless.

"I suppose," I answered carefully.

"How long were you together?"

"Almost four years," I sighed, gazing out over the breaking waves.

"Was that what you were crying about?" I took a long swallow of wine.

"Yes."

She was silent for a long moment, looking deeply into my eyes. I tried not to flinch away from her gaze, but I didn't want her to see the pain in them. Finally, she glanced away. Her voice was softer than I had ever heard it.

"You must have loved her very much." I felt a lump in my throat and swallowed hard.

"Yes, I did."

"Has there been anyone like her since then?"

I looked her squarely in the face, thinking what a strange question it was. "No. There never will be."

"That's too bad," she responded, turning her attention back out over the water. I felt uncomfortable and paced away to the corner, leaning on the rail.

How could she understand? I wasn't even certain I understood. I had a Master's degree in social work, I was a certified mental health counselor, and I wasn't at all sure why Caroline's memory kept me so detached from my lovers. That was probably why I had about two a year, kept them for four or five months, then ran like Hell.

There was one girl I had stayed with for a little over a year, but it had been a long distance relationship, and when she had moved to Seattle it had fallen apart rather quickly.

"I can't complain about my life," I said to fill the silence that stretched between us. "I've got everything I need, or could ever want." Who was I trying to convince?

"What about love?" I turned and stared at her. She was studying her wine glass, and raised a questioning face to me.

"I got enough love from Caroline to last me a lifetime," I replied, finishing my wine to cover the taste of the lie.

"Somehow, I don't believe that," she said, then drained her own glass. "I'm sorry. It isn't any of my business. I was just curious."

"Would you like another glass of wine?" I wanted to pretend that we had not had the discussion. It had been surprisingly easy to talk to Jennifer about Caroline, but I felt the conversation was straying a little too close to my personal problems.

"Sure." I took her glass and went inside to refill it. Melissa waved at me from over a steaming pot of shrimp.

"How's it going out there?"

"Just peachy," I grumbled. "I'm beginning to think you put her up to something."

"And what's that supposed to mean?" She put a hand on her hip and held up the spoon she had been stirring with like a weapon. I shrugged.

"She's just been asking some interesting questions, that's all."

"I'll be out there in a couple of minutes," Melissa called as I started back out the door. Jennifer had her back to me, gazing off up the shoreline toward the Oak Island lighthouse. There was a freighter entering the river, its stacks seeming to sprout out of the trees as it steamed past the island on its way upriver to the port at Wilmington. In all the years I've been there, I've never gotten used to the sight.

"Here you go." She turned back to me and accepted her glass. Her eyes were soft as she gazed at me, and I felt the beginning of a problem between my legs. *Damn, why does she affect me this way?*

"Thank you. You know, I envy you."

"What?" I blinked rapidly a couple of times. She sighed and leaned her back against the railing.

"You've known what real love is. All I've got to show for twenty-seven years of life is a battered heart and a few psychic bruises."

"My heart isn't exactly intact, Jenn," I said, shortening her name instinctively. Lines crinkled around her eyes as she laughed.

"Jenn. I like that. Mary used to call me Jenn."

"Mary?"

"An old girlfriend." I didn't pay much attention to her usage of the word. It's a common way of describing female friends in the south, and women don't think twice about using it in a non-sexual way.

"Well, I'm glad you like it. You just don't strike me as a Jennifer." She laughed again, more heartily.

"Thanks. Can I call you Kate? Or better yet, how about Kat? You remind me of a cat, the way your eyes shine in the moonlight." She gave me The Smile and I had to sit down.

What in the hell is she up to? I opened my mouth to respond.

"Hi, ho, gals. Dinner is served!" Melissa appeared from the house with a steaming bowl mounded with bright pink-red shrimp. I jumped up to help her bring out the salad and bread. Jenn sat where she was and watched my every move, her eyes burning holes into my skin.

"Saddle up to the table, Jennifer," Melissa said, pointing to a chair. Jenn slowly rose and strolled over to her seat. I glanced at her face and felt a rush of heat.

She knows exactly how she's affecting me! My jaw almost fell open when I realized it. She saw in my expression that she had been caught and put a polite smile in place of the one that was causing me so much trouble.

"This looks delicious, Melissa," Jenn said sweetly, sitting down. Melissa beamed. I wondered how so worldly a woman as my dear roommate could possibly miss The Smile. It lit up the entire house.

"So, Katherine tells me you have a gallery," Melissa said as she passed the salad. Jenn nodded and the two became engaged in a discussion of the modern art movement. That was fine with me, as I was feeling flustered and off-balance.

Jenn had been flirting with me.

She knew I was a lesbian, and she had still been flirting.

I'd had straight women flirt with me before, but I'd never reacted like this. Their flirtations had been just to see if I would bite, and I never did. I don't sleep with straight women. I leave initiations up to someone else.

What if Jenn is a lesbian too?

Even if she was, I wasn't going to allow myself to get involved with her. I couldn't. She was a nice, sweet girl, and I wasn't about to hurt her again. She seemed to have had enough of that in her life. I liked Jenn too much to start something that could only end in heartache for her. I knew I wasn't capable of committing to a relationship. If things started to look too cozy, I ran like a scared rabbit. I didn't want to hurt her like that.

But then, if she wasn't a lesbian, and she'd been hurt by men, she might be hoping I'd show her it could be different with a woman. That was even worse.

"Kat? Hello, earth to Katherine ...." I jumped and turned to Jenn. A faint smile wreathed her lips. "Melissa was just telling me about your collection of nudes."

I shot a startled glare at Melissa, who was innocently salting her salad. "What about it? I collect statuary. Big deal."

"I have a few pieces you might be interested in."

"Too bad I won't be in Raleigh any time soon." She looked momentarily taken aback, then shrugged and reached for a plate of shrimp.

"Katherine!" I ignored Melissa's disapproving face and got my own plate of shrimp. I had decided the best policy would be to subtly discourage Jenn.

The rest of the conversation at dinner was polite and fairly bland. I steered away from anything remotely pertaining to my love life. By the end of dessert, we were into a discussion of college football. Jenn and I were taking the position that the Carolina Tarheels were the best team in the country while Melissa stood staunchly behind her Washington Huskies.

"I'll help clear," Jenn said as Melissa got up to take in the dishes. I sat back and let them clear the table, knowing I would be doing dishes later. They returned and sat back down, and we looked at each other for a quiet moment.

"Well," I said. "What now? Cards? A walk?"

"I should probably head home," Jenn said unexpectedly. I smiled a little. My plan seemed to be working.

"So soon?"

"Yeah. I've had a wonderful time." I got up with her and walked her to the back door. Just as I was about to open it for her, she turned and took my hands in hers. "I'm sorry if I stirred up old memories, Kat."

"You didn't," I responded, trembling slightly. I liked the sound of my name falling from her lips.

"Good." She leaned over and brushed her mouth across my cheek before pushing the screen door open. "See you tomorrow."

V.

I stood and watched her walk down the stairs. As she vanished from sight, I gave a short sigh.

"My, you got quiet all of a sudden," Melissa said from behind me. I turned and looked at her.

"Didn't you see what she just did?"

"I guess I didn't." I sighed again and went to the kitchen to start the dishes. Melissa followed me, leaning against the counter.

"She kissed my cheek."

"So? That seems to be a universal thing around here." I shot her a dirty look.

"She was flirting with me."

"Sure she was," Melissa laughed. "She's just a very kind person, that's all."

I ran soapy water over the plates and grumbled to myself. Melissa stood at the counter and watched me. After a while, she stopped giggling and grew very still. I glanced over to see her studying me intently.

"What's your problem," I asked.

"You. I've never seen you like this. You're a wreck."

"I am not." She shook her head.

"I've seen you in the throes of lust before, Katherine, but this beats everything." I stopped washing and turned to face her.

"Okay, so I find her physically attractive. I find her wonderful to talk to, pleasant to be around. She's also straight."

Melissa folded her arms across her chest and lowered her head so that she was gazing at me from under her eyebrows. "Are you so sure of that?"

"If she wasn't, she would have said so by now."

"Mm-hmm." I didn't respond to the smug tone in her voice, and finished the dishes in silence. After a few moments, she went into the other room and left me alone. I was glad; I didn't want her to know the thoughts that were running through my mind.

*   *   *

I stood on the upper balcony, looking out at the moon's reflection on the water. Beside me on the railing sat a glass of wine, the last of the second bottle we had opened at dinner. I leaned my elbows on the rail and let the breeze caress my face, scanning the beach below me.

I saw her again.

She walked toward the water as she had before, her dark hair blowing in the breeze. She turned to me, her lips moving.

"Katherine." The name came to me like a soft kiss. It was Caroline's voice, the voice she used to say my name in after we had made love. There was more, but a sudden gust caught the words and they tumbled away from me.

I fought the urge to run down to the beach as I had done the first time, continuing to watch the apparition with a shuddering heart as she turned and walked into the water. She dove into the waves and vanished.

I stood alone once again.

The Carolina coastline has more than its share of ghost stories, but I don't think any of them deal with seeing one's dead lesbian lover. I didn't know what to think.

After a still, long time, I finished my wine and went inside.

I felt like Caroline was trying to tell me something, something that I couldn't – or wouldn't – hear. I got into my bed and turned out the light, and stared up at the ceiling for a very long time, my thoughts drifting between Jenn and Caroline, Caroline and Jenn.

Was my heart still so full of Caroline that there was no room for the burgeoning emotions I felt for Jenn? Or had Caroline's death left me so hollow that nothing could fill me again as she had, and had I given up trying? I could discourage Jenn all I wanted, it didn't change my feelings toward her. It didn't change the aching desire that lurked just beneath my skin, breaking free at the least provocation.

If Jenn was a lesbian, and I thought I really should just come out and ask her if she was, it would be all the more difficult for me to control myself. Despite the number of relationships I've had, I'm not into casual sex. Making love to Jenn when I knew fully well that we had no future together was something I wasn't prepared to do.

Regardless of what my mind was thinking about Jenn, my body was telling me that it would be a real fight should the occasion ever arise where I had to chose between heart and head.

Rolling over, I buried my head in my pillow and tried to clear my mind. All I wanted to do was sleep.

*   *   *

I did not see Jenn the next day after all. Instead, she called to tell me that her mother insisted that they go into Southport for the day. I tried not to let my relief show, and promised that we would go horseback riding the day after. I hung up the phone and turned to Melissa, who was sitting at the table nursing her coffee.

"I think I'll take today and catch up on my work," I said. She nodded absently. I noticed that she was starting to look tanned, and that it set off her hair quite nicely; in Seattle, city of eternal rain, the only tans you saw belonged to people who liked to lay under lights at tanning booths and tourists.

"Okay. I expect your phone bill is going to be about as big as the national debt by the time this vacation is over."

"Well, cellular service isn't cheap."

"Yeah." She laughed, then took a sip of her coffee. "I'm going to take some photographs. I thought I'd take the bike."

"Fine with me." I poured myself a cup of coffee and joined her at the table. Picking up the remote, I switched on the television and found CNBC.

After breakfast I drove down to the post office and got my papers, then returned to the house and spread out my work across the table. Then I logged onto my online broker and got some information on a couple of stocks that looked good.

John Inabinet stopped by to invite me out to dinner, but I politely refused, using the pile of paperwork in front of me as an excuse. After he left looking a little puzzled, I sat back and wondered if I would have turned Jenn down if she'd been the one to show up.

No, I wouldn't have.

Late in the afternoon I took a walk down the beach, relaxing the muscles in my neck which were tight and sore from sitting hunched over my computer all day.

Melissa and I went to the restaurant at the Marina for dinner, then rode back to the house. We watched a movie I had rented at the chandler's then turned in. I thought as I drifted off to sleep that it had been the first nice, normal day I'd had since I'd arrived.

*   *   *

I met Jenn at the stables the next day at nine-thirty. She had arranged for us to borrow two horses from a friend of her mother's, and the groom had the pair saddled and waiting for us.

Jenn's mount was a tall bay with white stockings, and mine was an appaloosa.

"How was your day," Jenn asked as she swung into the saddle. I put my foot in the stirrup and shrugged.

"I got a lot of work done. How was your trip into town?"

"Boring. Mother drives me crazy."

I tried to smile at her. "Then why subject yourself to her for the entire summer?"

"Because it's either that or miss coming down here all together." She gave me a grin. "I'll put up with a lot to get my addiction for this place satisfied."

I followed her out of the stable area and we took a trail that led us deep into a 600-acre undeveloped area set aside just for trails. Jenn was apparently a frequent rider, as she seemed much more at ease in the saddle than I. The last time I had been in the saddle was several months earlier, with a girl who thought it would be a good way to get to know me. She got to know me, all right. We broke up two months later, and she went back to her ex-partner.

Jenn and I rode for a few minutes just enjoying the warmth of the sun filtering through the trees and the sounds of birds. I had hoped to see some wildlife, but there was no sign of any.

"Did you enjoy dinner the other night," I asked finally. "I was a little abrupt toward the end of the meal, I know."

She shrugged. "I wasn't surprised. I was kind of prying into your personal life, and I shouldn't have been. I'm sorry."

"No, it's okay. Anything you want to ask me about Caroline is fine. I suppose I should be glad to have someone who knew her to talk with." I wasn't certain what prompted me to say that, but it was the truth. Jenn glanced back at me, and then dropped back so that we rode side by side.

"I'm more interested in why you haven't gone on with your life since she died."

"Have you ever seen someone die?"

"No," she answered quietly.

"I saw Caroline die. And I blamed myself. I still do." I couldn't believe I had just admitted that to her. Melissa was the only one I had ever told.

"I thought she drowned." Jenn's lips were drawn down in a faint grimace, her eyes narrowed slightly.

"She did. We'd been drinking."

"Oh. That's why you don't drink like you used to?" I nodded, looking away.

"That's part of it. I should have seen that she was in trouble. I should have gotten to her sooner. I was just too unsteady on my feet." Tears misted my eyes. Jenn was silent for a time.

"So you haven't let yourself love anyone since then?"

"No."

She looked me dead in the eyes, unblinking. "Then you're about the most selfish person I've ever met."

"Excuse me?"

"You're attractive, you have a wonderful personality, and you're smart. And you've kept all that for yourself and someone who's been dead for almost fifteen years. I was here that summer, I know what happened. Everyone knows what happened. Caroline had epilepsy. She went swimming and had a seizure. You couldn't have stopped that, and keeping all that blame to yourself is damned selfish."

I reined my horse in and stared at her. "What do you mean, she had a seizure?"

"Father talked to her father. He said Caroline had a grand mal seizure in the water. Yes, the alcohol probably contributed to it, but not as much as you're making out."

"Why do you care?" I started forward again, and she trotted a few steps ahead of me.

"I like you," she answered simply. "I'd like to think there was a chance you liked me."

"I do like you," I said, confused. She didn't reply, and we rode again without speaking. I was lost in my own thoughts. I had known Caroline had epilepsy, but I'd always thought it minor. Petit mal seizures took her sometimes, and she would stare into space for a moment or two, but never anything noticeable.

Why didn't anyone tell me that she had a seizure in the water?

Because I had been so hysterical over her death that my parents had put me in a private mental home for six weeks, and told everyone that I had decided to take a semester off of school to travel and get over it. They never mentioned her to me again.

Come to think of it, I never mentioned her to anyone but Melissa after that, either. ' No one had known that I blamed myself, or they might have told me about the seizure.

Had I spent the last fifteen years blaming myself for something I couldn't have prevented? The thought was unsettling and I tried to put it out of my mind. Regardless of the reason, she drowned, and I wasn't able to help her.

"Oh, well, as least I'm not the only one this summer."

Her words jerked me from my thoughts and I looked up at the back of her head.

"What?"

"I said, at least I'm not the only lesbian on the island this summer, for a change." When I didn't respond, and I couldn't because my airway had suddenly closed up, she stopped and turned in her saddle to look back at me. "Good Lord, I thought you knew."

"You haven't said anything ...." I managed. She was a lesbian. Desire bloomed full in my belly, sending shocks of warmth throughout my body. I tried not to blush.

"I've only dropped about a dozen hints."

"I've been a little wrapped up in my own problems, sorry." She was gay. If she knew I wanted her, there was a chance she would want me too. She had almost said as much just a few minutes earlier. My mind ran away with me, my heart starting to pound.

"Yeah, that's okay. It's been nice having you and Melissa around this summer. The last two years have been real bears. Mother wouldn't let Sue come with me either time."

She had a girlfriend. I felt a pain in my gut.

"Sue is ...?"

"Was. She decided that it wasn't worth the hassle. I hear she's engaged to some nice young man from Charleston now."

"So your parents know?" Jenny gave me a lopsided grin.

"They've never proven a damn thing. Mother just makes it difficult for me on principle."

I nodded. I never told my parents, but somehow they figured it out. It may have had something to do with the month I spent at that very exclusive rest home with my veins pumped full of tranquilizers following Caroline's death.

"How long have you known?"

"Since I was thirteen." I made the connection rather quickly.

"Oh. You mean to tell me ...." She nodded.

"It was you and Caroline. You were so happy together. I still remember the day I heard you in the lighthouse. I used to climb up there to get away from my family, you know. I was halfway up the stairs when I heard you two."

I blushed.

"The way you talked to each other, the way your voices sounded, sent shivers down my back. It explained a few questions I'd been having about my own sexuality." She let her mount walk a few steps and sighed ruefully. "I was jealous as Hell of you two."

"You know, you've had me at quite a disadvantage the past week." Jenn laughed.

"Oh, you mean the flirting." I nodded. "I'm sorry it was so obvious. I can't control myself sometimes. At first I was afraid you were with Melissa and she'd pound me into a bloody pulp before I could get myself under control."

"And after you found out I wasn't with Melissa?"

"Well, that's harder to explain." She shifted uncomfortably in the saddle and looked away. "You're a remarkably beautiful woman, Kat. I thought so when you were twenty, and I think so now. I find you very attractive." She turned her gaze back to me, our eyes meeting and locking. I forced myself to not tremble at the look of desire on her face. It was easy to recognize now.

"Jenn ... I'm not someone you want to be involved with."

She sighed and urged her horse to walk. I followed suit.

"I can't help the way I feel, Kat."

Would hearing her call me that always make me tremble?

"It would never work out."

"How do you know?"

"Because," I replied, choosing my words carefully. "I still belong to Caroline. I always will." She didn't say anything. "It isn't that I don't find you attractive."

"You don't think I'm too big?"

I laughed. "Jenn, with a body like yours I wouldn't be concerned about my weight. It's all muscle." The braid of her ponytail fell back over her shoulder as she flipped her head.

"I'm not very pretty."

"I think you're striking." She smiled back at me.

"Thanks. I have trouble with women who expect me to be butch because of my size. I'm really not."

"I've never understood that butch/femme thing," I said. She nodded.

We continued our discussion of butches and femmes for the remainder of our ride, but my mind was only half on what was being said. The rest of me was examining the past fourteen years of my life.

If what Jenn had said was true, and Caroline had drowned because of a seizure, then nothing I could have done would have saved her, and I shouldn't have spent all those years blaming myself.

And if I shouldn't be blaming myself, then what reason was there for me to continue hanging on to her memory?

Because I loved her so completely that I was afraid I'd never find something as perfect again. And yet, a few paces in front of me rode a woman who made me feel almost the way Caroline had. I felt I could connect with Jenn on a level that I had never been able to connect with any of the women I'd dated since Caroline.

We returned to the stables after a few hours, and gave our animals over to the care of the groom. I felt strangely wiped out, as if I had run all the way we had ridden. I just wanted to go home and take a long nap.

"Listen, Kat," Jenn said as we walked to our golf carts. "I was wondering if you'd like to have dinner at the marina with me tonight."

"No. I'm sorry, Jenn, I can't. I'm feeling very confused right now, and I think it might be best if I just went home and tried to sort my life out." Her shoulders slumped a little and she tried to hide her dejection, not very successfully.

"Okay. I understand. I hope this doesn't mean you're going to start avoiding me."

"I'm not going to avoid you." She grinned at me.

"Good. Then how about tomorrow?"

"We'll see. I'll call you in the morning."

She nodded and put her hand on mine, giving it a squeeze. "I hope you think of me as a friend."

"I do. I really do, Jenn."

* * *

It rained that night, one of those driving thunderstorms that rush in off the ocean with lightning flashing and thunder rolling and waves crashing, in our case crashing at the steps leading up to the deck. I took two sleeping pills instead of one, and dropped off into an appropriately drugged sleep just as the storm reached its zenith.

I drifted into a dream about Jenn. We were walking along the beach as we had done my first night on the island, but we were holding hands. I felt a fullness in my heart that I thought I was incapable of knowing.

The sun was shining down on us as Jenn slipped her arm around my waist and led me up toward the dunes. In the soft loose sand above the storm line, she turned to me and bent her head to kiss me. I felt my body responding, filling with need as her lips worked across mine.

But something was wrong.

I felt as though there was someone I should be looking for. I pulled away from her and turned back toward the ocean. She reached for me again, but it felt wrong.

"Kat, I want you," Jenn said, slipping her arms around my waist from behind. I kept scanning the waves, knowing that there was something I was missing, something I should know.

I heard nothing.

I saw Caroline.

She was floating just beyond the breakwater, face down in the blue-green. I tried to break free from Jenn's embrace, but she held me firm.

I fought, struggled against her arms, screaming Caroline's name. Finally, Jenn released me and I ran down the beach toward the water, tearing at my clothes, my shoes. A powerful dive sent me through the waves, and I swam with all my might toward the body floating limply just beyond my reach.

I reached Caroline and turned her face up. Slipping an arm around her ribcage, I pulled her toward the shore, struggling against the undertow and the waves that tried to drag us out to sea. It seemed like forever before my feet found bottom and I staggered out of the ocean, my arms under Caroline's. She didn't move.

I laid her down on the sand, her long black hair streaming out around her pale face. I bent over her and started to perform CPR on her.

One, two, three, breathe. One, two, three, breathe. I turned my head to listen for her breath. There was none. Up the beach, by the dunes, I could see Jenn, standing with her arms crossed watching me.

Why wasn't she helping? Caroline needed help!

One, two, three, breathe. One, two .... On and on it went, with no reaction. I felt her chest beneath my hands, tasted the salt water on her lips. But she was gone.

Finally, I sat up. A wave broke near us, the water running up around Caroline's legs, dragging sand out from under her body. I felt the tears on my face and reached down to touch her hair.

She opened her eyes.

As I stared at her, her lips moved.

"Katherine, let me go," she breathed.

I woke up screaming.

VI.

I heard footsteps on the stairs leading up to the loft and Melissa came barreling into the room. She pulled up short and stared at me. I was shaking, sweating, crying and screaming all at once. Without a word, Melissa crossed to the bed and took me in her arms.

Feeling her gave me an anchor to reality, and I tried to shake the dream from the edges of my vision. I buried my face against her neck and held her tightly. Melissa is the only person alive that I would allow to see me like this, would allow to comfort me the way she was.

We were never lovers. That is one reason we get along so well together. I met Melissa at the University of Washington when I went there to start my masters program. We had hit it off immediately, and had become something beyond friends in the years since. But there had never been a sexual attraction between us. She wasn't my type any more than I was hers. And that allowed me to trust her with a physical intimacy that I would never allow a lover to have.

She held me until I had stopped crying, and then brushed the wetness from my face with the edge of her nightshirt.

"Better?" She asked. I nodded quietly. "That must have been a bad one."

"She spoke to me." Melissa reached out and switched on the bedside lamp.

"She what?"

"She spoke to me. She told me to let her go."

Melissa frowned. "Has she ever done that?"

"No." We both knew we were talking about Caroline, but Melissa knew as well that I wouldn't want to hear her name so soon after the nightmare had ended. "Jenn was in it, too."

I explained the dream to Melissa, who listened gravely, looking into my face the whole time. When I had finished, she shifted her gaze to a print of sailing ships in harbor which hung on the wall above the bed.

"Do you want me to tell you what I think?"

"Not really," I replied. "I'm pretty sure I know already."

"You're feeling torn between your love for Caroline and your desire for Jenn. Which is only natural."

"I told you I didn't want to know." She smiled at me.

"When has that ever stopped me?"

I growled something and let her go. "You're irritatingly perceptive sometimes."

"Well, that's true. Has she finally come out to you?"

"You knew about her?" Melissa laughed and stood up. I pulled my knees up to my chest and wrapped my arms around them. Outside, the storm was abating.

"I had a good suspicion. You know I don't like to pry into your life, Katherine – "

"Bullshit," I exploded, trying not to laugh. "It's your favorite activity."

"But I think the two of you would make a good couple."

All of a sudden, I wasn't in such a humorous mood any more.

"I'm not looking for that kind of trouble, Mel."

"Your problem is that you consider it trouble," she responded with a wry smile. "I would consider it a gift from the goddess."

"I don't believe in a goddess," I growled. Melissa just shrugged and headed for the stairs.

"Then you have a lot of thinking to do, don't you."

She wasn't kidding. I sat in bed and stared at the wall for a while, trying to sort through the emotions running rampant in my body. I had a feeling it was going to be a long night.

*   *   *

"Good morning," Melissa chirped when I dragged myself downstairs. I threw her a dirty look and went in search of coffee. When I returned to the table, she continued in her sweet voice, "Did you sleep well?"

"You know damn well I didn't," I growled in reply. "I was pacing all night."

"Well, at least you look like shit." I pursed my lips and debated dumping hot coffee in her lap. She saw my expression and didn't continue.

"Did you decide anything?"

"Yes," I said. I had finally decided that I wasn't strong enough to go through this trouble for the rest of the summer, and I told Melissa so. She listened gravely.

"When are you going to tell Jenn this?" I shrugged. "Soon, I hope."

"Maybe I'll take her to dinner tonight. I don't know. This shouldn't be happening to me, Mel. I've spent all this time building an impenetrable wall and in one short week I feel like its all falling down around me."

"Is that a bad thing?" Melissa spread cream cheese on an English muffin and took a bite, looking at me with a raised eyebrow. I sighed and blew on my coffee.

"You know, all that psychological crap is great as long as you don't have to apply it to yourself."

Melissa laughed. "No shit, Sherlock."

I got up and wandered toward the front sliding doors. The storm had blown over, leaving a crystal bright morning behind. The deck was still wet with rain, and a couple of chairs had blown over against the wall, but other than that, there was no damage. I went outside and leaned over the railing, looking down at the seaweed wrapped around the bottom steps. The water had come up to the second riser.

I hoped we didn't have a hurricane while we were there, because I doubted the house would survive it. I debated calling a moving company right then and arranging to have the place emptied out, and finding a condo to rent for the rest of the trip.

"Hey, are you going to the post office today?" Melissa called from inside. I turned my back on the ocean and squinted in at her.

"Yes, after I finish my coffee."

"I have a letter for you to drop off." I wandered back in and took the envelope from her. It was addressed to Belinda Trenton.

"Again? Why don't you just call her?"

"I have been. I'm sorry, I miss her." I shook my head in mock disgust and Melissa laughed. "You're a real jerk, you know that?"

"I try, sweetheart."

*   *   *

The Smith Island post office is a building about as big as my garage in Seattle. There's hardly enough room in the area where the mailboxes are for three people to turn around in. As I walked in, there were two women checking their boxes and a man with a package at the window. I dropped Mel's letter through the slot and went to my box.

I pulled out my Wall Street Journal, Investor's Business Daily, the Zweig Report, and two letters for Melissa, then turned to leave, almost running into Jenn in the process. I thought instantly of my resolution not to get involved with her. But instead of being strong, I felt myself wanting to take her in my arms and hold her.

I started to turn white.

"Hi," she said.

"Hi," I returned, swallowing. She held a pile of envelopes which she dropped through the slot, her eyes never leaving my face. "I was going to call you this morning."

"Well, it's lucky I'm here then." She smiled and my stomach gave a disquieting heave. It was easier to not be attracted to her when she wasn't standing right in front of me.

"Let's go outside."

Outside, I shifted from one foot to the other, chewing on my lower lip nervously. I glanced at the chapel across the street, then decided it wasn't private enough for the discussion I wanted to have with her.

"Kat, you don't look so great. Are you feeling okay?"

"I had a long night last night. I did a lot of thinking." Her face went blank, but I couldn't tell why.

"Katherine ...." She paused and I waited patiently for her to continue. Her eyes moved from my face to the lighthouse over my shoulder. "Let's go into the lighthouse."

I felt a cold wash of outright fear. "No. I can't."

"They've completely restored it. You won't hardly recognize it, I promise." I turned and looked at the tall gray spire.

"But it has a lot of memories I don't need right now."

"I think maybe you do." Her voice was soft, yet held an insistent tone that I found hard to resist. I gazed at the lighthouse for a moment longer, then shrugged.

"Okay. But I can't guarantee how I'll react." She started walking purposefully toward the door at the base of the lighthouse with me in reluctant tow. Pushing the door open, we stepped into the gloom.

It had been restored. New stairs spiraled up into the darkness, and the interior had been replastered and painted white. I drew in a deep breath. Jenn went to the bottom of the staircase and put a foot on the first step.

"Come on. We'll talk at the top."

"I don't think this is a good idea, Jenn." She turned to me with a faint frown.

"What are you afraid of, me?"

"No, of course not."

"Then come on." I followed her up the stairs, watching the gentle sway of her hips until I was almost hypnotized. Caroline had been a very slender girl; when she walked there was almost no movement of her hips, but Jenn's swayed back and forth with a delicious motion.

After a long climb, we stood on the top floor of the lighthouse. A door led outside to the walkway, and windows circled the walls. The remains of the spotlight stood in the center of the room, roped off with a plaque set in the floor by it. I looked around and tried to picture making love to Caroline here; it was difficult. It looked so much different.

"Well?" Jenn was looking at me expectantly, her arms folded easily across her chest. I turned my attention to her.

"It isn't as bad as I thought it would be." She smiled.

"That's what I figured you'd say if I got you up here."

I walked over to the door and looked out. I could see over the river side of the island from there, the marina and its buildings and the condominiums that were being built on the far side of the harbor. Across the river, I could see Oak Island.

"Jenn," I began. She made a noise and I turned back to her.

"Look, Kat, I can see how it is. I just want us to be friends. Do you think that's possible?"

"Well, of course it's possible." She smiled and came toward me with her hand out. I steeled myself to shake it.

"I'm glad." Her grip was firm and businesslike. I looked at our clasped hands and wondered how I could have ever gone so weak in the knees over something so ordinary.

Then I met her gaze and saw The Smile. I froze.

"Jenn ...." All my desire rose at once and overwhelmed me. The curve of her lips was inviting me to take that one step that would put me into her arms. I swallowed hard, trying to look away. She grew puzzled.

"What's the matter?"

"Are you doing that on purpose?"

"Doing what?" She frowned, her eyes darting across my face with concern. "What am I doing?"

"Looking at me that way."

"What way?" She obviously didn't know about The Smile. I dropped her hand and turned away, my mind spinning. I had come close to kissing her then, too close. "What did I do, Kat?"

"Nothing. You didn't do anything." I crossed my arms against my chest, hugging myself against the ache in my body for her. She was silent behind me.

I felt swirls of emotion eddying through me. I shivered, fighting to maintain my self-control. Then, with a suddenness that startled me, my thoughts were clear. I turned back around and faced her. She was staring at the floor, her hands clenched, arms ramrod straight against her sides, her entire body a portrait in confusion.

"Jenn, look at me." She shook her head. I took two steps and cupped my hand under her chin, raising her face. I looked at her for a long, silent moment.

"I don't understand you," she said. I managed to smile, studying her lips.

"I don't either."

It was so easy to kiss her then. I pressed my mouth to hers, feeling the sudden breath she took through her nose as I ran my tongue lightly around her lips. She opened to me, soft wetness, our tongues touching in the dark warmth. Her arms lifted around me as mine encircled her waist, and we stepped together, pressing the full length of our bodies against each other as the kiss grew deep.

Caroline had never been further from my thoughts.

Jenn's mouth was expressive, questing and hungry. I found myself surrendering more to her than I had planned, more than I wanted. My fingers ran up her back and along the planes of her shoulders, a moan starting in the back of my throat.

Her hands slid under my shirt, and started up my sides. I felt her fingers gently brushing against the sides of my breasts, forced myself to break the kiss, gasping with desire.

"Oh, Katherine," she breathed, her eyes still closed. I felt my heart pounding against my ribs, felt the hardness of my nipples and the swelling ache between my legs.

"Jenn, I ...." I couldn't speak any more. We kissed again with passionate abandon. I moved my mouth from hers long enough to kiss her eyes, her cheeks, her chin. She moaned, pressed against me. I felt the hard points of her nipples against my chest.

My hands slid down, cupped her hips, pulling her to me. She groaned unintelligibly, running her lips across my face and neck. Her fingers caressed my belly, my sides, the small of my back where my waist curved into my jeans.

I was wild with desire, aching with the rush of warmth between my legs. I wanted her hand there, to feel her moving with me in the primal dance.

I heard voices on the stairs.

Abruptly, we broke apart, taking hurried steps away from each other, running hands through hair, tucking in shirts, grinning like idiots at one another.

It was a group of women. They had cameras and video recorders and were being led by one of the members of the Smith Historical Society, the island's version of a park ranger. The voice I had heard belonged to him.

He looked at us.

We looked at him.

I moved toward the stairs first, laughing a little. Jenn followed me, and we moved past the group giggling like teenagers. About halfway down the stairs, it hit me, how close we came to discovery.

"That was close," I said.

"You're telling me," Jenn laughed. "Made me feel like a kid again." She moved beside me and took my hand.

"We shouldn't have," I responded simply. "I shouldn't have given in."

"And why not?"

"I'm not ready for this." Jenn looked over at me and sighed. "I'm sorry, Jenn. I'm just not ready for how I feel."

"How do you feel?"

"Confused."

"At least you're honest," she said dryly. "That's more than I can say for most women."

"I need to think about what happened, about this." She was silent. We reached the bottom of the stairs and went outside. I stopped and turned to her. "I'm very attracted to you, Jenn. I just don't know that I can handle a relationship with you."

"Come to dinner tonight. We'll talk."

"I don't know ...."

"Don't make me beg."

I managed a smile. "Okay. What time?" We agreed that she would pick me up at eight, then shook on it and went our separate ways. I drove back to the house in a daze, still able to feel her lips on mine, to see her face before me.

Melissa wasn't in the house when I arrived. The front slider was open so I assumed she had gone down to the beach. I switched on CNBC and got a soda out of the refrigerator, then collapsed onto the couch and stared at the ticker.

Everything I had decided the night before, all my pacing and worrying, was out the window. I had resolved to keep my relationship with Jenn on the footing of a friendship, to not give in to the desire in my body. And the first thing I had done was fall into her arms.

Running a hand over my face, I drank from my soda then set it down on the table, reaching for a notepad to jot down from quotes. I couldn't allow what had happened between me and Jenn to affect our friendship. I would have to sit down at dinner tonight and tell her that.

I doodled absently on the paper as I watched numbers slide past on the television screen. Jennifer Brooks was an outstanding kisser. Her lips and tongue had set me on fire, a fire that I could still feel smoldering in the pit of my stomach. All it would take was another dose of The Smile to send me right over the edge into a full-blown conflagration.

National Western Life Insurance was up a point and a quarter. I went to note that on my pad and saw what I had been doing while my mind was busy elsewhere. Scrawled across the paper were various combinations of my name and Jenn's.

I stared at the pad.

"Cute," Melissa's voice came over my shoulder. "Where are the little hearts with the arrows through them?"

"Shove it, Mel," I grumbled. "I was just doodling."

"Interesting doodles. You know, I've read that a person's doodles say a lot about them. These say a certain Kate Jenkins is preoccupied with a certain Jennifer Brooks."

"Shove it," I repeated, tearing off the paper and crumpling it. Melissa laughed and moved off toward the kitchen. She had on her bathing suit and Birkenstocks. I thought it interesting how easily she had taken to the environment. This was a woman who passed up every chance I ever offered her to take off to the Washington coast for a weekend.

"So where've you been?" She came back with a glass of tea.

"I ran into Jenn at the post office. We talked."

"And?" She leaned against the back of the couch and took a sip of her drink.

"And none of your business."

Melissa laughed. "In other words, you either proposed to her or wish you had."

"Smart ass. Neither. But we are going out to dinner tonight."

"Dear, you look like the cat who ate the canary." I checked my expression and corrected it. But it was too late.

"Okay, we went up in the lighthouse. I got carried away and kissed her. But I'm better now." I reached for my Coke Cola.

"You're better now? Not bloody likely."

"I don't want to hurt her," I said honestly. "I won't let myself get involved if it will hurt her."

"Well, that's refreshing." I glared back at her. "Hey, I've seen how you operate."

"Oh, go away and leave me in peace." Melissa laughed and pushed off the couch, heading for the door. I looked back at the television and started making notes again.

VII.

I wore a long cotton skirt and sleeveless mock turtleneck to dinner. I brought a cardigan with me in case it got chilly. Jenn picked me up right on time, wearing a pair of dark purple slacks and a cream blouse. I offered her a drink to take with her, but she politely refused. I had the feeling that she didn't want to come in and face Melissa's scrutiny, and when we were in the cart and en route to the marina, my suspicion was confirmed.

"Did you tell Melissa what happened?"

"Not exactly."

"Oh. Well, I expected you would. You two seem to get along very well together."

I laughed. "Lots of practice."

Jenn nodded and smiled. We chatted about nothing in particular during the drive, and I for one felt the tension between us. I knew she wanted to kiss me, and I wasn't going to let that happen again. I couldn't.

Parking in the lot at the marina, Jenn helped me out of the cart and escorted me up the steps to the restaurant. We were seated behind a red-faced older man and a younger blonde woman with three small girls.

I gathered from their conversation that the man was the grandfather and the woman the mother. The girls were remarkably well behaved, albeit a little loud, but the woman seemed intent on getting drunk, and I was glad that they appeared to be almost through with their meal.

"So," Jenn said after we had placed our cocktail orders. "I suppose we might as well jump right in. You're going to tell me to get lost, right?"

"Why do you assume that?" She smiled ruefully.

"Because every time I feel this way about someone nice, she tells me to take a hike. I don't exactly attract 'keepers'."

I rearranged my silverware. "I'm not going to tell you to take a hike. I want to have you as a friend."

"Almost as bad."

Our drinks arrived, and I busied my hands with the little umbrella that came in mine, opening and closing it, twirling it between my fingers, anything to discharge some of the nervous energy I felt. Behind me, the blonde woman was starting to argue lowly with her father over something.

"Tell me how you met Caroline," Jenn said abruptly. I stopped twirling the umbrella and looked at her. "I mean, was she your first?"

"Yes." I heard the man mutter something with the word 'lesbians' in it, and the woman return angrily 'so what?' A moment later, they rose and gathered the children together and left. I sighed in relief. "I met Caroline at summer camp."

"Summer camp?" I nodded.

"We were junior counselors together. We had similar interests and just sort of hit it off. We used to canoe over to the inn and get drunk on the free wine over dinner."

The inn across the lake from our camp served wine free by the carafe with meals because it was a dry county and they weren't allowed to sell it. Therefore, since it wasn't being sold, they never asked either of us for any ID.

"Sounds romantic."

"It was. But nothing happened there. After we got back, we started visiting each other. She lived in Raleigh, so we drove back and forth, talked on the phone, all that sort of teenage stuff. One weekend, she stayed with me in Greensboro while my parents were down here. We broke out a bottle of my dad's wine and drank it, and made love on my bed."

"Weren't you terrified?"

I nodded. "I wasn't a virgin. But I knew no boy I'd ever kissed had made me feel the way I did when Caroline leaned over and planted her lips on mine. I knew I'd wanted her to for a long time, I just hadn't known it until then."

The waitress interrupted us to take our order. I asked for a dozen oysters on the half-shell and the pompano, and Jenn ordered soft shell crab. When the waitress left, I continued with my story.

"It seemed so natural for us to want each other. I'll never forget how I felt the first time she touched me. We made love all night long."

"I didn't make love to a woman until college," Jenn said.

"I thought you said – "

"Oh, I knew all through high school. But you know how it was at GCD; I doubt there was another lesbian within five grades of me. The ten percent rule certainly doesn't apply at that place. Except for the teachers, maybe. You heard about Ms. Carver and Ms. Antoinne?"

"No. Really? I always had suspicions about Ms. Antoinne, but Ms. Carver?" Ms. Antoinne had been my tenth grade history teacher, a wonderful woman who inspired me to explore feminism in my college years. Ms. Carver was the chemistry teacher, and I'd always thought she was just too damn mean to get married.

"You bet. Mister Tredwell walked into Ms. Antoinne's office one day and found the two of them in a … compromising position, shall we say?"

I had to laugh. Gentle Ms. Antoinne and heavy-set, grumpy Ms. Carver? I had no doubt who was the butch in that relationship.

"So they got fired, huh?"

- 82 -

"Not exactly. Carver was all upset and Antoinne told Tredwell where he could put it for walking in without knocking. Then they both quit. I run into them now and again at one of the bars in Raleigh."

"So you had to wait until college, huh?" Jenn nodded.

"I decided to go to Randolph-Macon because I figured the odds would be better. Besides, I recognized a bit of man-hater in myself and I didn't want to put up with a bunch of frat boys hitting on me at Duke."

"And I guess you were correct about the odds." I sipped my drink and looked over at her. She seemed so young and full of energy. She made me feel old.

"Yeah. It took some subtle maneuvering, but I found the network before the end of my first year. Unfortunately, like I said before, I don't have very good sense when it comes to women. I got my heart broken a lot."

"And after school?" She laughed and finished her Tom Collins.

"I got my heart broken by a wider variety of women. I've been pretty much out of the dating scene this year, since Sue dumped me. I was beginning to think it wasn't worth it."

The waitress came back to refresh our drinks and bring the appetizers. We chatted about past lovers over oysters on the half shell, then sank into a silence while waiting for the entree. I couldn't help but think how nice Jenn looked, how much she had filled out since she was thirteen. She had gotten an interesting outlook on life, too.

Our dinners arrived, and she took a few bites before glancing up at me with questions in her eyes.

"What is it, Jenn?"

"I suppose it would be old fashioned to ask you what your intentions are."

I grinned. "It would be old fashioned, though a bit strange, if your father asked me what my intentions were."

"I'm serious."

"What can I say? I'm not the type of woman you want to get into a relationship with. I'm the type that runs the other way the minute things get serious."

Jenn studied me critically for a long moment. "Why?"

"Why do I run? Fear." I cut into my fish and didn't look at her. I didn't want to see her face.

"I don't understand you, Kat. I don't understand what makes you tick. Are you really happy with your life?"

"Yes." I didn't want to complicate things with a longer answer. Yes, I was happy with my life, what life I had. I had Melissa to keep me company, and the occasional lover to satisfy my physical needs. It was a cheater's way of living and I knew it. But I wasn't able to do anything differently.

"Suit yourself." She attacked her food. After a while, she looked up and caught me watching her. "You're a damn good kisser, though."

I blushed. "Thanks. I've had enough practice, I ought to be. You aren't too bad yourself."

"Yeah, well, fat lot of good it does."

"Jenn, try to understand. I don't want to hurt you. I like you too much to do that."

She snorted. "I'm over eighteen, I can take care of myself."

"That isn't what I'm trying to say."

She paused, then relented. "Okay. I'm sorry, Kat. I've had a serious crush on you since I was thirteen. It isn't easy for me to accept defeat. I didn't expect you to carry me off into the sunset, but I was hoping to at least make it to bed."

I narrowed my eyes and looked at her. "I'm not into one night stands."

She shrugged. "I take what I can get."

"You deserve a lot better." I toyed with my fish, then felt her watching me and glanced up at her. Our eyes locked, and I saw into her soul for just a moment. What I saw there tore at my heart. I was hurting her, even by trying not to, I was. "Damn, why does life have to be so complicated?"

"I don't know," she responded quietly.

"I really do like you, Jenn."

"Oh, stop saying that! I don't care if you like me. It's beside the point. Maybe you can pretend that what happened today was just one of those things, but I can't. It meant something to me." She hurled the words at me in a voice that stung me with its quiet calmness.

"Fine. So what am I supposed to do about it?" She looked taken aback for a second.

"Come off your high horse. Admit the possibility that there might be something between us if we let it happen."

I was perfectly willing to admit that. "But I can't let it happen, Jenn." She sighed.

"Well, it's better than nothing I guess."

I looked over at her and felt my heart leap. She was so innocent looking that I wanted to hold her and comfort her and tell her everything would be all right. Even if it was a lie. I wanted her like I'd wanted no other woman in my life.

Even Caroline.

The thought was like a bolt of lightning down my spine. I stiffened, staring at Jenn. She saw the change in me instantly, her face growing concerned.

"What in the – "

"Nothing."

"That's not what your face says."

"Jenn ... I ... I can't. Oh, shit, I'm really sorry." I couldn't think of anything else to say, and turned my attention to my meal, painfully aware of my flaming cheeks. Jenn didn't speak again, and we finished eating in silence.

The ride back to my house was strained. I stared out my side of the golf cart at the darkness and wished I could make everything better for both of us, and knowing that I couldn't.

Outside my house, I turned and looked at her, wanting to kiss her goodnight, not daring. I put out my hand.

"I'll see you later," I asked hopefully. She looked at my hand, then at me. Her face was set hard against obvious pain.

"You're one cold woman, Katherine." I let my hand drop and got out. She drove off before I was even halfway up the stairs.

*   *   *

Melissa was waiting up for me. She looked over from the couch when I came in and lifted her hand in a half-hearted wave. I grimaced at her and went to change into my nightshirt.

"I take it things didn't go too well," she said when I came back out of the bathroom, rubbing my face.

"That's an understatement. I think I managed to alienate her sufficiently. I wish I thought that was a good thing."

"Ah." I paced across the floor, then back.

"Damn. All I was trying to do was tell her gently that I didn't want to hurt her."

"Katherine," Melissa said in a severe tone. "I don't think that's something you should have done. She's the one to decide if she wants to risk getting hurt."

"That's what she said. I just wish I didn't have these feelings for her. I'm so damned confused ...."

"Sit, Katherine, talk to your friend Mel." I came over and sat next to her. She put an arm around my shoulders and patted my knee, which made me feel about a hair better.

Slowly, I related the evening's events. Melissa nodded sagely and made no comment until I was done, when she withdrew her arm and stood up, looking down at me.

"Katherine, sometimes I wonder just why I'm friends with you. Especially when you start acting like a jerk. She as much as told you she didn't expect a lasting relationship, and you turned even that around on her."

That really stung. I looked up at her, my eyes wide. "I didn't mean ...."

"Didn't mean doesn't matter. What difference does it make if it only lasts a month? Why is she any different from the dozen other women you've dated?"

"She's different. I can't explain it, but she is." Melissa blew out her breath and threw her hands up in the air.

"Oh, I surrender. You are bent on destroying any chance you have of happiness, all because of something that happened fifteen years ago. That's nuts. It's beyond nuts, it's insane! Caroline is dead, Katherine. Get over it!"

"Don't you talk to me like that. Not in this house. Not where it happened. I'm not ready to get over it. I'm not ready to get over her!" I turned and stormed upstairs, tears filling my eyes.

*　　*　　*

I spent the next day miserably moping around the house. Melissa wasn't speaking to me, and it was a weekend, so I didn't even have the tickertape to watch. I read my magazines, studied the paper, and moped.

I had slept fitfully, and tired as I was, I couldn't bring myself to lay in that bed in the loft and stare at the ceiling trying to nap. Dinnertime came, and went, and finally I had no choice but to go to bed.

The next day was a repeat of the previous one. Everything I tried to do reminded me of Jenn, of her voice, her laugh, her eyes, her lips .... Finally, I couldn't take it any more. I dialed her number and listened to it ring.

Her mother answered the phone and told me to hold while she rounded Jenn up. I felt my heart in my throat as the seconds clicked past, then I heard her voice.

"What do you want?" She sounded tired.

"I need to talk to you."

"What else is there to say, Katherine?" I swallowed my heart and bit my lip.

"Please. Come over and let me apologize." There was a long silence. "Jenn?"

"You want to apologize."

"Yes. I was wrong. Rude and wrong."

"Okay, Katherine. I'll be over in a while." She hung up and I replaced the receiver in its cradle, staring at it for a moment.

What am I going to say to her face to face?

It didn't matter, as long as I saw her again. I had come to realize that I not only wanted her, I needed her. If that meant having an affair that I knew from the start would be over at the end of the summer, so be it.

I changed into more appropriate clothes, slacks and a pullover polo shirt, and settled into the couch to wait for her. She arrived half an hour later, looking about as haggard as I felt.

"Come in," I said quietly, opening the screen for her. She slipped past me and stood just inside the door, waiting. "Do you want something to drink? Tea? A beer?"

"Tea, please." I poured two iced teas and we sat on opposite ends of the couch.

"Jenn," I began.

"Katherine," she interrupted. "I was out of line the other night. I was trying to force something on you that you obviously weren't ready for. I'm sorry."

"And I was acting like a jerk for no good reason."

"Well, where does that leave us?"

I sighed and took a swig of tea. "Jenn, what happened in the lighthouse ... it isn't something that happens to me. I don't lose control of myself like that. I don't let desire for a woman get under my skin until I have to do something about it. At least I didn't until I saw you."

"Stone butch, huh?" I laughed at her reference, but the laughter was a little forced.

"No, I'm not a stone butch. Not by far. I just don't let myself get involved with women that deeply. Jenn, I find you more than just attractive. I ... you scare the Hell out of me."

She seemed surprised, and I wondered why. I thought it should have been apparent that I had been running since the moment I found out she was interested in me.

"I scare you? In the name of the Goddess, why?"

"Because of what I feel when I'm around you. Because you make me want to forget ...." I trailed off, staring at the floor. She finished for me.

"Caroline." I nodded. "Oh, Kat."

My voice was soft. "I want you so badly it hurts, Jenn. But I know our time is limited. We're both too old for a summer romance." She set her tea down and reached out to take one of my hands in both of hers. I hadn't noticed how large and warm they were before, but they engulfed me and held me tightly.

"Kat, I don't think either of us is ready for a long-term relationship. Maybe neither of us ever will be again. I don't care about that. I just want you for as long as I can have you. That's all. A summer romance may be just the thing for both of us right now." I looked up at her, seeing her tender eyes.

"Jenn," I whispered my need.

Her eyes lowered to my mouth. I didn't flinch away when she leaned in to kiss me. I felt her lips on mine and melted into them, tasting her with my tongue. Her hands released mine and moved around my waist, pulling me across the sofa to her lap.

Our kiss went deep, tongues meeting, twining, parting to explore one another. I felt the softness of her inner cheeks, her hard, even teeth, then again the liquid fire of her tongue against mine. I ran my fingers through her hair, wanting it loose, wanting to feel it falling against my face when I bent to her breast. I was alive with hunger, rational thought fading away.

"Oh, Kat ...." she breathed into my hair as I moved my mouth to her neck. Her hands slipped under my shirt, setting my skin on fire. "I want you ...."

I kissed my way down her neck to the curve of her shoulder, then across the V of her shirt. I could smell her cologne and taste the salt of her sweat on my lips.

"Not here," I whispered, kissing her mouth lightly. "Mel is down on the beach."

"No, she's not," Jenn returned, starting to pull back from me. I opened my eyes and saw her looking over my shoulder. Slowly, I turned and saw Melissa coming up the stairs.

"Damn." I started to slide off of Jenn's knees, but she dropped her arms to my waist and held me. Melissa came through the slider, looked at the two of us on the couch, and smiled broadly. "Uh, Mel ...."

"I'm glad to see the two of you made up. I suppose I'd best make myself scarce for the afternoon. Expect me back around five, Katherine." She went into her bedroom. Jenn kissed me again with a long leisurely tongue before Mel came back out with a blouse and shorts on. With another grin, she grabbed her camera bag and headed out the back door, mouthing the words 'See you at five'.

"She's a very considerate room mate," I explained nervously, lest Jenn think Mel was accustomed to finding me in this sort of a position. Jenn laughed softly, her hands tracing along my thighs suggestively.

"I'm glad. Shall we go upstairs, or do you want to risk another, less understanding, interruption?" I stood, taking her hands in mine as I pulled her to her feet. I was trembling with nervousness and desire, half afraid she would change her mind.

"We don't have to do this if you aren't ready ...."

"I've been ready since that night I saw you at Janie Millikan's." She smiled at me, not quite The Smile, but close.

"Upstairs, then."

VIII.

I was aware, as I led the way up the narrow stairs to the loft, that it was the first time I had shown Jenn my room. My heart was pounding with anticipation, and at the same time I felt strangely awkward. The loft was open to the living room on one side, with only a railing dividing it from the rest of the house. I stepped aside to let Jenn up onto the landing, hoping she wouldn't feel too uncomfortable with the open airiness of the room.

The ceiling and walls were of whitewashed pine board, the ceiling slanting from a height of perhaps ten feet at the railing to five feet at the outside wall. The sliding door out to the balcony was inset in its own gable. Besides the double bed there was a large dresser, a rocking chair, a three-shelf bookcase and a small writing table.

I gestured to all this with a grand sweep of my arm. "This is it. The guest room, my parents always called it."

"It's absolutely fabulous," Jenn gasped, walking a few steps forward. "I never knew this house had a balcony. You can't see it from the beach."

"No," I agreed. "It's set into the slope of the roof too well. It's a very private place, I used to spend a lot of time out there."

"I like it." She turned and held out her hands for me to take. I did, and she led me to the outside doors. "I want to kiss you out there, under the sun. May I?"

I shrugged. "I suppose. No one can see us." I unlocked the door and pushed it open, letting in the sound of the sea and the smell of the hot sand. We walked out onto the balcony and stood just shy of the railing, looking out over the water.

"I'll bet the sunrise is dazzling from here."

"Yes." I stepped to her and slid my arm around her waist. She turned into the embrace, lifting her hands to my shoulders.

We kissed, softly, tenderly, almost a chaste kiss. The next one was anything but innocent. It took my breath away, her mouth on mine, her tongue teasingly running along my lips, flicking at mine, dipping into my warmth. I felt weak in the knees, and tightened my arms around her to keep my balance.

Finally, I pulled my lips from hers and took her face in my hands, moving across it with tiny kisses. I smelled her musk, her shampoo, all of her, and wanted all of her. She dropped her head back as I reached her neck, growling deep within her throat at the myriad of tender nibbles I took on her skin.

Her hands moved up my sides, caressing the curve of my ribcage, the softness of my breasts, then pulled me against her tightly, so that the top of her bosom was pressed against the fluttering pulse of my neck. I could hear her heart beating in her chest.

"Let's go in," she murmured. "Now." I led her back inside, closing the door with my foot. We stood apart, looking at each other, and I saw my own hunger reflected in her glowing green eyes.

Slowly, I reached up and undid the barrettes holding her hair up out of her face, then lifted the masses of sandy-blonde strands and let them cascade over her shoulders. I love long hair; the tactile experience of it slipping through my fingers is as arousing as a kiss. Jenn stood still while I ran my hands through her long tresses, then suddenly reached up and caught my wrists.

She very deliberately lowered them until my hands were at the top button of her blouse, my palms resting just lightly on her breasts. "I can't wait any more," she said, her voice husky with desire. I undid her shirt slowly, gently, kissing the skin exposed as each button fell away. She wove her hands into the back of my hair, caught fistfuls of it, murmuring my name.

Her bra fastened in the front, and I slipped the hook apart, running my fingers along the underwire to lift it away from her breasts. Then I slid both blouse and bra off her shoulders with one movement. She dropped her arms and the clothes fell to the carpet.

She stood naked from the waist up, gloriously tanned and muscled except for two creamy white triangles over her breasts, each marked with a heavy rose-brown nipple. If not for that full bosom, she would have looked like a body builder.

I studied her for a scant moment, then bent my head to capture one of the hardened nipples in my mouth. Jenn drew in a sharp breath and pressed forward against my lips. "Oh, yes, Kat...." I ran my tongue around the rigid bud, suckled at it, then kissed my way across her chest to claim the other one. "Goddess, yes ...."

My fingers found the buckle of her belt, unfastening it. Underneath, the clasp of her slacks, the zipper, fell open to my touch, and I put my hands one at each front pocket and slipped the pants down her legs. She pushed her sandals off and stepped out of her slacks, and when I raised my head from her breast, she stood before me in only a pair of high cut pink cotton underwear.

Her hips were wide, her thighs thick. I suppose some men might say she was a little broad in the beam, but she looked heavenly to me. She had dancer's legs, or perhaps rider's, firm thighs, well muscled, strong calves. The slight curve of her belly told me that she didn't worry about dieting, that she wasn't concerned about the board-flat stomach modern society seemed to think women should have.

"Do you approve?" I looked up and caught her concerned look, and nodded emphatically. "I warned you I wasn't skinny."

"Darling, you're perfect." She sighed and let go of my hair, running her fingers along my jaw.

"I had a girlfriend tell me I should lose about fifteen pounds."

"From where? What lesbian in her right mind wouldn't want you just like you are?" That brought a broad smile to her face and she raised my head so she could kiss me.

"You're sweet. Now, what do you look like under there?" She finished pulling my shirt out of my pants and lifted it over my head, dropping it to the floor beside her, then went onto her knees and reached behind me to unfasten my bra. I looked down at her, saw the delight in her eyes when she at last freed my breasts; I'm pretty proud of them myself. A lesbian obviously didn't write the old saying 'more than a handful's a mouthful and more than a mouthful's too much'. While not as big as Jenn's, I've never had any complaints about them.

Jenn wasn't any different. She put a hand on the outside curve of each breast, pushing them together. and pressed her face into my cleavage. Her tongue ran a wet, warm line up toward my throat, then back down and around each nipple in a slow circle. I moaned, feeling the gush of wetness between my legs as her mouth claimed first one, then the other. She used her tongue well, first lapping softly, then hardening and flicking at the tip. Her teeth closed gently around each nipple, scraping upward. I shuddered.

I couldn't wait any longer. My hands went to my slacks, but she knocked them away and unfastened my belt herself, her mouth never leaving my breast. I helped her pull down my slacks, kicking off my Birkenstocks and stepping out of my pants so that she saw me in my French cut Hanes briefs.

I remembered the tattoo and wondered what Jenn would think of it. I wondered if she would even notice it. She sat back on her heels and studied me head to toe. "Wow."

"I'm a little out of shape," I told her ruefully. She shook her head, running her hands up my legs.

"Not that I can tell." She kissed me at the bottom of my ribcage, then ran her tongue down to my belly button. It tickled and I laughed.

And stopped laughing abruptly as she moved down and pressed her mouth at the Y of my legs. Her hot breath stirred through the fabric of my briefs, sending a shock of desire exploding through my body. "Oh, Christ ...."

"You smell wonderful," Jenn said, her voice muffled by my body. She sat back and stood up. "I can't wait to taste you."

I went weak again. Jenn took my hand and led me to the bed. Reclining across it, I drew her down on top of me, feeling her weight fully against my body. She was heavier than I expected, but it felt good to be pressed into the mattress. We lay groin-to-groin, breast-to-breast, looking into each other's eyes.

Jenn bent her head and kissed me, at the same time pressing her hips forward into mine with a gentle yet insistent motion. I spread my legs wider, allowed her to slip between them. I felt her nipples pressing against me, her hands, on either side of me palm down on the mattress to support her weight, were still just brushing my back.

"I've wanted you for so long," she whispered, pushing against me in a slow rhythm. I lifted my arms around her shoulders and pulled her fully against me, tilting my hips up to meet her. My underwear was soaked through. I wanted to feel her against my skin, touching me.

"Take these off," I ordered, moving my hands down to her waistband. She got up on her knees and complied with the instruction, then reached out and slipped mine down over my hips and past my thighs, allowing me to kick them the rest of the way off.

Her hair was blonde, silky and thick. I could see the silvery wetness in it, and sat up with her, reaching my hand to her, wanting to touch her. She stopped me. "Not yet."

"Why not?" A slow grin lit her face. She pushed me back across the bed and spread my legs wide, bending my knees so that I lay with my soles on the mattress.

"Because." She slipped down and nuzzled at the top of my red triangle. I dropped my head back and moaned. She moved her mouth down the insides of my thighs, back up, blowing gently into the wet curls but not touching. Her hands slid to the joints of my legs, rubbing small circles just at the edge of my hair.

"Don't tease," I pleaded. She glanced up at me with a smile, then spread my lips with her fingers and dropped her head. Her hair fell across my belly and thighs as her mouth captured me. I arched my back, and she moved forward, her tongue searching, tasting, lapping at me, teasing. "Oh, so good ...."

She caught my clitoris between her teeth and flicked at it with her tongue, then began long strokes that spread my lips and brought shudders through my body. Her hands released me, then slid under my buttocks, pulled me to her.

If I'd had any doubts that she had been with women, she would have erased them then; she brought me to the teetering edge of orgasm and held me there as I begged and pleaded with her. Her hands came up to my breasts, capturing my nipples between each thumb and forefinger. She held me for a long moment, then sent me spiraling into oblivion with a single flick of her expert tongue. I screamed her name, arching on the bed. She stayed with me, her mouth on me, taking the wetness that came from me in wave after wave until I collapsed, limp.

Jenn crawled up beside me and took me in her arms, kissing me softly. I tasted myself on her lips, felt one more shock run through me. "Oh, Jenn." She kissed my shoulder.

"Thank you," she said simply. I wanted to take her right away, but my body wouldn't respond. I had to rest. I lay in her arms, feeling her fingertips tracing up and down my shoulders, my upper back, my arms and legs and stomach.

After a few minutes, I felt my energy returning. I turned in her embrace and kissed her, my mouth telling her that I was ready. She rolled onto her back, bringing me across her stomach. I kissed my way down her chest, kissing her nipples, my fingers seeking out her tangled wetness. She spread her legs for me, lifted her hips to my cupped hand. I molded myself to the shape of her, dipped my fingers into her hair and felt her shudder as I gently spread the lips of her labia. She was wet, ready.

"Tell me what you want," I breathed, feeling her moving beneath my hand. She spread her legs wider.

"Inside – two fingers," she replied in a ragged voice. I pressed against her, feeling her pulling me in as I followed her request. I moved so that I lay between her legs, my hand pressing into her warmth, feeling her responding with a trembling need. I wanted to taste her badly, and slipped down to add my lips to my fingers. She wove her hands into my hair and offered herself to my mouth.

I wanted to make her wait, but she was too ready, too hungry. I felt the orgasm gathering inside her, and took her to it, moving with her faster and faster until she bit back a scream and locked her thighs around my ears and came. I took her until at last she pushed me away with a shuddering sob, then crawled into her arms and kissed her. She lay with her eyes closed, her hair spread out like a halo across the rumpled sheets, her chest heaving as she fought for breath.

"You're wonderful," I said, snuggling next to her. "Absolutely wonderful." She responded by squeezing me, then reached over and pulled the blanket, which had fallen on the floor at some point, up over us. We fell into a quiet, satisfied reverie from which I aroused some time later. I looked across the pillow at Jenn's face, relaxed almost into sleep.

"What is it?" Her voice was almost a whisper. She opened her eyes and looked back at me, unblinking.

"You're beautiful," I replied. "I just wanted to look at you."

She stretched languorously and ran a teasing hand up my spine, smiling when I twitched away from her fingers. "You're beautiful, too."

"I mean it, Jenn. I guess I shouldn't, but I can't help remembering you at thirteen, all legs and knobby elbows ...." I traced along her firm, muscular arms. "You looked like a boy. You certainly don't any more."

"You don't look the same either, Kat. I like your hair short. When it was long, it made your head look too heavy, like your neck wouldn't support it."

"Thanks," I laughed and pressed up against her, wanting to feel the warmth of her skin against mine. She responded by rolling onto her side, her softness against mine. I felt her breath in the hair behind my ear. "Be careful, you might start something."

"This would be a bad thing?" She responded, hugging me. I shook my head and smelled her fragrance. Desire rekindled in my stomach.

"Not at all." She met my kiss tenderly. Our second coupling was long, slow, gentle, building toward explosive climax, our lips never parting as our hands caressed and played and sought out the sensitive parts of one another's bodies.

Afterwards, we lay on our backs, staring at the whitewashed ceiling. I was softly caressing her still-quivering thigh with one hand, the other tucked up behind my head. "I wish I could stay all night," Jenn mumbled.

"I'm sure your mother wouldn't approve," I chided in a teasing tone. She smiled over at me.

"I'm sure she wouldn't."

"So, was it what you expected? After fourteen years, I'd think reality would be something of a let down." I looked at her, saw her grinning.

"It was better than I expected. I didn't think you'd be this uninhibited. I always saw you as a little strait-laced."

"I'm anything but straight," I said, making a face at her.

"I'm glad." She put a hand over mine and squeezed.

We snuggled together and watched fluffy white clouds floating past the window on the opposite wall. After a bit, I suggested a shower, and we went downstairs to the bathroom.

I talked Jenn into letting me shampoo her hair, luxuriating in the feeling of the soap and her tresses moving under my fingertips. We washed each other, kissing and playing under the stream of water until it started to run cold, then stepped out and got dressed.

When Melissa returned, we were sitting on the couch sipping tea. She came through the door and grinned at us. "Have a good afternoon," she queried.

"Yes," I said nonchalantly. Jenn nodded, a ghost of a smile wreathing her red-brown lips. "How did your photography go?"

"Just fine. I saw that doctor – what was his name, Inabinet? – on the way home. He seems quite puzzled that you aren't falling all over him. He sort of quizzed me about you."

"What did you say?"

"Oh, the usual; you're a diesel dyke who's into S&M with animals, that sort of thing." She ducked the pillow I threw at her. "Actually, I told him you were dating someone. You are, aren't you?"

"That's better." My mock indignity faded. Jenn and I exchanged glances, and she just barely tilted her head to me. "Yes, I'm dating someone."

"Good. I'm glad to hear it." Melissa grinned again and went into the kitchen for a beer. Jenn glanced down at her watch and jumped up.

"Goddess, it's almost five thirty! I've got to get home – I told mother I'd only be gone a little while." I stood with her.

"Lunch tomorrow," I asked.

"Twelve noon. Meet me at the grill." I walked her to the door and kissed her softly on the lips. She looked at me momentarily, then swept me into her arms and delivered a real lip lock. "Damn, seven years older than me and she doesn't know how to kiss a girl good-bye. Talk to this woman, would you Melissa?"

"You got it, Jenn." Jenn kissed me again.

"I don't want to leave."

"I don't want you to." She hesitated at the door.

"This is silly," she finally said. "I'll see you tomorrow."

After she had left, I waited for a minute or two before turning to face Melissa. "Well, you can guess how it went."

"Quite well, I assume. No details, please. This is one time I don't want to know." She was leaning against the column at the end of the breakfast bar, sipping a Corona.

"I hope I'm not making a mistake."

"Yeah, well, just remember that in life the only failure is not trying." I screwed up my face and stuck my tongue out at her.

"Oh, great fount of wisdom. How would I ever survive without you?" Melissa shrugged.

"You wouldn't. You'd shrivel up and die."

"You, my dear, are a smart ass."

"And you, sweetheart, could light a city the size of Seattle with the afterglow you're putting off. I haven't seen you this happy in years."

I looked at her, trying to decide if she was serious. Then I took a look inward, and realized that I was happier than I had been in years. The warmth I felt didn't come from just the first time making love with a new woman; there was something deeper to it. It made me nervous.

I returned to the couch and sank onto it, leaning forward to rest my elbows on my knees. Unabated desire was something I could handle; I'm accustomed to it. But what I felt went beyond desire, beyond the rekindling of sexual interest.

How far beyond? And how far would I let myself fall before I started to run away?

*　　*　　*

The stock market opened down twenty points Monday morning. I had gone to the post office and retrieved my chart books and was busily drawing lines in them with red and blue pens to check for patterns. The red pen was for highs, the blue for lows. I watched for breakouts, slow-downs, or other signs that a stock was ready to move higher or lose value.

I already had a list of twenty or so stocks that I wanted to investigate when the market opened, and when I saw the downturn, I immediately phoned Jean to sell off a couple of holdings I felt were particularly vulnerable.

Melissa came in from her morning walk with a sunny smile. "Hiya, Katherine."

"Hi. What're you so happy about?" She shrugged.

"It's a beautiful day. You know, I'm beginning to think I've been missing something by not going to Copalis with you."

"You have been. But Copalis Beach is nothing compared to this, if you ask me. You know, you're looking really good." She smiled more broadly.

"I've lost eight pounds," she announced. "Belinda isn't going to know what to do with this tanned, sleek goddess when she sees me." I laughed.

"You've only got two more weeks to survive, dearest. Try not to be so glum." She threw me a dirty look which I caught with innocent eyes.

"Hey, just because you aren't doing without isn't any reason to rub it in. I might just decide to fly back early. Poor Belinda's all alone in Seattle surrounded by all those predatory bar dykes she hangs around with." I tried to imagine Belinda having to fend someone off, and failed.

Mel's girlfriend is five foot six, about two hundred pounds of solid shipfitting muscle, and as innocent as a Hell's Angel. She works at the Bremerton shipyards as a welder. Sometimes I wondered what she and Mel saw in each other, but I did know that they read Shakespeare to one another, and from what I've been unable to avoid overhearing, they both enjoy pretty rambunctious sex.

Melissa didn't have Belinda stay over too often, and I tried to not be there when she did, but every once in a while I had no choice. The only thing to do then was put in my earplugs, turn up the stereo, and dig out a trashy novel.

"I think she'll survive," I told Melissa, who did her best imitation of a flounce as she left the room. Shaking my head, I returned to my work.

"How did you sleep last night?" She asked me from the bathroom, letting me know that she wasn't really mad at me.

"Like a baby."

"Any dreams?" I coughed. I'd had a dream, all right, but it wasn't the kind she was asking about.

"No. Do you think we can swing a dinner party on Thursday? Angela Millikan is leaving Friday and I think we ought to have her over before she goes."

"Sure. I suppose that means Janie and Roger, too." Melissa rejoined me and plopped down in the chair next to the couch.

"Yep. I'll grill steaks." We settled into a discussion of the details for the meal, then I went over and called to invite the Millikans. Janie said yes, of course, they'd love to come, and we set a time. Glancing at my watch as I hung up, I saw that it was time to get ready for lunch.

Jenn was waiting for me on the steps outside of the grill. She broke into a big grin when she saw me pull up and dashed down to meet me, sweeping me into a hug before I was completely out of the golf cart.

"I missed you," she whispered. I set her gently back.

"I missed you too, Jenn. But, Christ ...."

"Sorry." We went inside and got a table that looked over the eighteenth green. Jenn ordered a beer and I got iced tea, then we sat and stared at each other for a while, not exactly embarrassed, but uncertain. I didn't know what to talk about; I only knew that when she had touched me I had wanted to throw her to the ground and take her right in the parking lot.

"I'm having the Millikans to dinner on Thursday. Would you like to come?"

"I'd love to. Will you have dinner with me at the club dining room Friday?" I nodded. "I was hoping we could get together this afternoon."

"I'd like that." Jenn smiled, apparently satisfied that she wasn't going to be rejected after the previous day's activities. "I've got a serious problem thanks to you. As if I wasn't hot and sweaty enough from the humidity ...."

"I can take care of it as soon as lunch is over," she replied.

"Not too soon," I laughed. "We wouldn't want to get a cramp, now would we?"

We were at ease again, and chatted about statuary until our sandwiches arrived. Around a mouthful of egg-salad, Jenn dropped a piece of news on me.

"Lynne's coming down for a couple of weeks." I stopped chewing and stared at her.

"Lynne knows about me, doesn't she." Jenn nodded. "Does she know about you?"

"I don't think so. I don't really care, either. But I thought I'd better let you know, Mother's going to be wanting you two to get together just like old times." I swallowed and covered my lack of an answer by sipping at my tea.

"Interesting turn of events," I finally managed. Jenn nodded.

"Isn't it? Oh, well. I really enjoyed yesterday, you know."

"So did I." There was a moment of silence. "Let's drive up to east beach after lunch." Jenn agreed.

We finished our lunch and got into my cart. Once we were on the main road, Jenn slipped her hand across my thigh and smiled softly at me. I returned the smile and covered her hand with my own. The warmth from her fingers radiated through my skin and reached my groin, causing a dull swelling ache. I wanted to kiss her a thousand times, didn't dare on the wide-open stretch of road that we were traversing.

There are many narrow streets paved through the thick forest of the island, and most have no houses on them at all. The main roads run east-west and north-south, and in between meander these smaller pathways. Some aren't even maintained, having been paved during an earlier, more ambitious phase of the island's history.

When I had turned into the forest, I sought out the first one of these smaller roads and went far enough down it that I was certain we couldn't be seen. I stopped and locked the brake, then turned and looked deep into Jenn's eyes. Without a word, I moved my free hand into the hair at the nape of her neck and pulled her to me, tasting her lips as though for the first time.

When we parted, her breath came raggedly. She studied my face, eyes heavy-lidded, and kissed me again, her hands moving to my waist. Her tongue darted into my mouth, claiming me, sparking the desire I felt into a raging need.

I had only wanted to kiss her, to feel her lips against mine, but now I found that my body required much more from her. My hands sought out the softness of her breasts, cupping them through the fabric of her shirt, feeling the hardening nipples under my fingers as she moaned my name. I kissed her neck, her face, and her lips. I wanted her desperately. One hand dropped to her lap, sliding between her legs and moving forward ....

"Kat ... Kat, stop .... Oh, darling, you have to stop!" I finally sat back and looked at her, flushed with desire, confused that she didn't want me.

"What's the matter?"

"Logistics, darling. This isn't a '57 Chevy, and I'm not about to lie down on the ground right here with the bugs and the sand spurs." I glanced around. The ground was thick with fallen sticks and clotted vines. There wasn't anywhere to lie down.

"Then let's go back to the house." She shook her head and cupped my chin gently with her hand.

"Are you always this impatient? Wait until we get to east beach. There's miles of dunes there; nice, soft, sandy dunes where no one can see us."

"Yes. All right." I kissed her firmly once more and put the golf cart in motion. It took us ten more minutes to reach the cabana at east beach. There were several carts parked at the recharging station there, but no one was in sight. I plugged my cart in and took Jenn's hand as we climbed the steps to the cabana.

At east beach the dunes run inland for about one hundred yards before fading into the trees. We walked toward the point for about half a mile, then cut up into the dunes and selected a nice secluded spot. Jenn knelt down and held her hand up to me, pulling me down beside her.

"You've been a very patient girl," she murmured after she had kissed me. "You deserve a reward." Her hands were at the small of my back, pulling my shirt out of my shorts, running along my skin with teasing lightness.

I yielded to her, opened to her. She undressed me with deliberate slowness, kissing and caressing each new patch of skin as it came bare, then spread my clothes out on the sand and gently lowered me down onto them and came on top of me. Her fingers sought out the moistness between my legs, her hand molding to my body, teasing pressure.

My vision was full of Jenn, my thoughts, my soul, given fully to her lips, her fingers. She pressed into me with quiet determination, and began to move against me. I felt the tension building, my legs tightening. I wrapped my arms around her and held her to me, lifting my hips to meet the thrusting of her hand. Then I was falling, floating, clinging to Jenn as the spasms took my body.

She looked down at me with a tender smile. "Better now?"

"Yes," I responded raspily. "But I want more."

"You'll get more," she said, sitting up and pulling off her shirt in a sudden motion. I beheld her magnificence again, awestruck, then she was lifting me up to her chest, offering her breasts to me. I suckled greedily at them, trilling with pleasure at the sounds she made in her throat as my tongue moved across her nipples.

"Jenn ... I need ... want ... to touch you ...." I spoke as I moved my face between her breasts, my hands at her shorts. They came off in a flurry, and I brought her back down on my lap so that I supported her weight with my thighs, my hand between her legs, searching, exploring the wetness for the source of her raging heat.

I entered her and heard her long gasp of pleasure, and began to move into her, holding her against me with my other arm around her waist. She put her hands on my shoulders and clenched them there, ten spots of near pain from the strength in her grip. She rode me, I urging her on. "Come on, baby, come for me ...."

"Oh, Katherine!" She cried at last, throwing back her head. Her hands jerked from my shoulders to my neck, into my hair, holding me firmly as she writhed on my hand.

I held her as she came down from the climax, my cheek resting against her chest, feeling her heart beat. She was so much bigger than Caroline. My legs hurt from her weight on them. Caroline had been so light that I'd hardly ever noticed her.

This had been Caroline's favorite position.

Tears sprang uncontrolled to my eyes and I buried my face into her bosom and started to cry.

IX.

It took Jenn a minute to realize that I was crying, then she was on her knees beside me, cradling me in her arms. I couldn't control myself; the harder I fought, the more I cried.

"Kat – dearest – what's wrong? Did I hurt you?" I managed to shake my head. What could I tell her? I couldn't tell her the truth. It was unfair of me to be thinking of Caroline, when we had just shared a passion with which I was still shaking.

"I ... I'm sorry," I sniffled around the lump in my throat. Jenn was rocking me gently, kissing the top of my head. She felt warm and secure, and I realized I had never allowed a lover to see me like this.

Why was Jenn so damned different?

I had made love to women before exactly as I just had Jenn. I'd never reacted this way. Slowly, I got my control back; the crying slowed and stopped. I sat there in the sand, arms around Jenn, and let the thought I didn't want to admit go through my head; *I think I could fall in love with her.*

"Kat?"

"Yes, Jenn? I'm better. I – I don't know what ...." Jenn set me back and looked at me, shaking her head slowly. I sighed. "I can't help it, Jenn. She just comes barreling into my mind sometimes."

"Don't worry about it. I understand. Are you feeling any better?" I nodded. She smiled tenderly and kissed me. "Don't punish yourself. Come on, we'd better not push our luck." I stood and helped her to her feet then we brushed the sand off one another and got dressed.

We were well on our way toward home before Jenn spoke again. "After Caroline died, how long was it before you took another lover?"

"Three and a half years."

"What made you take one then?" I glanced over at her, my face turning red.

"I got drunk. Not one of my prouder moments. A group of us were out at this lesbian bar in Seattle and a woman I knew slightly was coming on to me pretty strong. I got drunk and went home with her."

"What happened after that?" Jenn was studying me, and I wanted to shrink into a ball and roll away. But, of course, I was driving and thus trapped.

"I found out two weeks later that she had a husband. Needless to say, I stopped seeing her." There was a noise from Jenn's throat.

"Do you often cry after sex?" I shook my head emphatically.

"Never. Melissa's the only person who's seen me cry. And now you, twice."

"I guess that means you like me." I stopped the cart in the middle of the street.

"I thought we had already established that I like you, Jennifer. That is hardly the point." Down the road I saw a cart approaching us, and started forward again. "You just remind me a lot of her."

"Who, Melissa?" Jenn's voice was puzzled.

"No, Caroline."

Jenn quickly stifled a laugh. "I'm sorry. How in the name of the Goddess do I remind you of her? I'm an Amazon and she probably weighed about a hundred pounds wringing wet."

"She weighed one eighteen. I'm not talking physically. I mean, inside, I guess. You're both artists, you both like long walks and sports, you have similar interests in books. You even like the same kinds of wine."

"I don't know that I like that." Jenn pursed her lips. "I want to be liked for me." We raised our hands in greeting as we passed the other golf cart.

"I'm not saying I like you because of her. I'm saying the reason I was crying is that you remind me of her."

"Oh." Jenn looked pensive.

"Come over tonight," I said. "I'll make it up to you."

"Can't," she responded, shaking her head. "Mother and Dad are having the Willoughbys over and I have to be there to entertain the twins."

"After?"

"Maybe. I have to play a little hard to get, after all." I smiled, glad that the mood had lifted.

"Well then, we'll play it by ear."

*   *   *

Jenn and I spent the rest of the week trying to fit each other into our schedules. Life on the island isn't hurried, but it sure is easy to get booked solid if you aren't careful. I hadn't realized how many places I had agreed to be until I tried to make time to be alone with Jenn.

And I didn't want to ignore Mel, who would be leaving at the end of the next week to head home. That meant that there were times when Jenn and I had to sit together in a room full of people and try not to let on that we really wanted to go back to my house, to my loft, and make love.

I was growing addicted to the way Jenn made love to me. She was a strong, determined lover, skillful and willing. But she was also sensitive to my needs and desires. She would quote poetry to me as we lay together in the afterglow, her voice a quiet cadence, hypnotizing me with its steady rhythm. Her authors ranged from Browning to Gertrude Stein.

She never stayed the night. I didn't ask her to, and I don't think she would have accepted if I had. I didn't want her to know that after she left, after I had finished replaying our day together, I would go to sleep and dream about Caroline.

I now dreamed about other things than Caroline's death, although that was the predominant subject. Sometimes, the two of us would be walking together, or sitting on the deck, talking. I never remembered upon waking what we had talked about, but I knew that we talked. She seemed so young to me now, since I remembered her as a twenty year-old girl. She seemed in some ways silly and childish to me. But still, I loved her.

Thursday morning dawned cold and windy. The sky was overcast, and the reddish glow of the dawn clouds made me think of the old adage:

Red at night, sailors' delight;
Red in the morning, sailors take warning.

I turned to the weather channel instead of CNBC, and looked at the tropical storm heading for the North Carolina coast. Mel came out of her room scratching her head and found me sitting there staring at the television with a sick look on my face.

"Problem?"

"Early season storm. It's headed for the coast. I don't think this place can stand up to a storm like that." Melissa looked around the room, then sat next to me and put her hand on my arm.

"How long until they know whether it will hit us?"

"Twenty-four to thirty-six hours. Christ, I can't get this place cleared out in that amount of time. What am I going to do?" About that time, there was a knock at our back door. Mel went to answer it while I stared at the television some more.

It was one of the Barney Fife's, as my father was fond of calling them, the private police force for the island. This particular officer was a slender woman about my height.

"Are you Ms. Jenkins?" I nodded. "May I come in?"

"Sure. Mel, go start some coffee, would you? Care for a cuppa, officer?" She nodded and smiled as Mel went into the kitchen.

"I see you've heard about Anatoli," the woman said, looking past my shoulder at the television. I nodded. "The boss wanted me to make sure you heard. You were supposed to be moving everything out of here at the end of the summer, right?"

"Yes. As you can see, I wasn't expecting a hurricane in mid-June." She laughed, a short, terse laugh but a laugh nonetheless.

"Who was? We've got a van if you want to take out your valuables, small stuff, the TV, that sort of thing. We'll keep it at the station until this thing blows over. And me and the others can help you board up after our shift if it starts to look serious." Mel rejoined us.

"Goddess, Katherine, I didn't realize how bad it could get."

"Even a tropical storm can have winds up to sixty miles an hour, Melissa. Imagine what the storm surge will be. Up a good three or four feet, and we don't have any dunes to block all that water. Even if the house doesn't fall in, the garage will be under water." Mel started to put her arm around me and stopped, looked at the officer, and dropped down onto the couch.

"I'll take advantage of that van, officer," I said.

"Please, call me Bert."

"Bert?" I looked this slender woman up and down. She looked like a cop, short hair, wiry frame, piercing blue eyes. She wore no rings. But she didn't look like a Bert.

"Bertha. I hate it. Or you can call me Collins, if Bert is too much for you." I exchanged glances with Mel, sitting where Bert couldn't see her. She mouthed the word dyke at me. I couldn't smother the grin.

"Bert's just fine. As long as your boyfriend's name isn't Ernie." She looked me square in the eye.

"I don't have a boyfriend." Emphasis on the boy. Behind her, Mel got up quickly and went into the kitchen before the twitching of her lips could erupt into laughter.

There is a time tested way of checking out whether one is talking to another lesbian. It isn't foolproof, but I've found that it works a good part of the time, especially in the south. Mel and I had checked our travel guide for women and found that there was a bar in Wilmington called 'Muses'. So, trying to sound casual, I leaned against the back of the couch and laid my trap for Bert.

"Mel and I were thinking of heading over to the mainland this weekend. Can you recommend a good place to shoot some pool or grab a couple of drinks?" Bert looked me up and down.

"I always go to Muses in Wilmington, but –" Mel's whoop startled her. "What the – "

"Busted," I drawled, smiling at her. "Member of the pink triangle club, eh?"

"Guilty." Mel came back with three coffee mugs. She handed one to Bert, and one to me, then leaned against the couch beside me.

"What is this, some sort of lesbian hideaway you haven't told me about, Kate?" Bert looked confused.

"We seem to keep finding family popping up," I explained.

"Well, you two were pegged before you left the boat," Bert replied. "Joe Blain couldn't wait to come tell me about you. I'd have stopped by sooner, but I had vacation, and we've had a real problem with raccoons this year."

"What did he say about us," I asked quietly, sipping at my coffee. I wanted to know if there was a rumor going around about me.

"Oh, he told me I had to check out the couple at the Jenkins' place. His gaydar was going wild, and you two had matched luggage, or something like that. Oh, and one of you kept calling the other 'sweetheart'."

"I told you to stop that," I said out of the corner of my mouth at Melissa. She shrugged helplessly.

"I can't help it. After seven years, it sticks. I'm not used to being in the closet." I sighed. "We aren't a couple," Mel said to Bert. "We just share a house."

"Oh. Well, whatever, you guys aren't alone. There's about a dozen of us this year, plus the weekers." Weekers are tourists who rent houses for a week or two.

"Well, we should have a party," I laughed. Bert nodded sagely.

"Except everyone's terrified if someone sees more than three of us together at the same time they'll know exactly why. Jeez, and I thought the army was paranoid."

"Oh, you haven't seen anything until you've seen a lesbian bank executive who's got a girlfriend in a law office," I replied. Bert laughed, and then looked at her watch.

"Hey, I gotta run. I'll send that van by this afternoon, along with a couple of fellows to haul the heavy stuff. Don't leave anything you don't want to lose." She drained her coffee and handed the mug to Melissa with a wink, then left. I turned to Melissa with an innocent face.

"Why, I do believe she likes you."

"Stuff it, Kate," Mel growled.

"She's your type."

"I said …." I laughed and shook my head.

"This is going to be interesting, having a dinner party and moving out at the same time." I sighed and looked around, picking out the things I wanted to move out.

It was like that mental exercise, if my house was burning, what would I grab? Photographs, paintings, the brass ship's wheel my father loved. Everything from the garage except maybe the washer and dryer. The cappuccino machine (I had sent this to my father a few years prior and was surprised to find it down here instead of at his winter house). The items I really wanted from the house were few and small.

What surprised me the most was that what I wanted the most couldn't be so easily moved. It was the house itself. I'd been able to handle the thought of purposely demolishing the place, but faced with the prospect of losing it to the ocean, I was ready to fly into a panic.

All the memories that I'd lose, all the laughter and the pillow fights, watching sports with my father, weekends with Caroline and other friends, even the memories of Jenn and the upstairs loft, all of these were things that I didn't want to live without.

"Katherine?"

"Huh? Oh, sorry Mel. I was just remembering all the good old times me and this house have had together." She came over and put her arm around me. I leaned my head against her shoulder and sighed.

"Nothing's certain until the instant replay."

"You and your witticisms," I growled, but smilingly.

The van arrived at three, along with two men who willingly hauled the television and the boxes of photographs, and all the other junk I had accumulated during the day into one pile in the living room, down the stairs. They had me sign a form, then told me to call if I needed any more help.

Jenn arrived at five. The Millikans, after calling to confirm that dinner was still on, would be there at seven. The weather forecast was still calling for the storm, called Anatoli, to hit Cape Fear at around one-thirty p.m. on Friday with sustained winds of fifty-three miles per hour and gusts of up to sixty-five. The storm surge was anticipated to be three feet, and coincided to within fifteen minutes of high tide.

Jenn strolled through the door as I was watching the latest update and tracking the storm on the hurricane chart we had always kept in the closet.

"Permission to come aboard?"

"Jenn!" I turned from my work and forced a smile. She saw the trouble in my eyes.

"It's bad, isn't it." I nodded. "Oh, I'm sorry, Kat." I rose and went to her arms, and let her kiss me. She was big and warm and sent relief surging through my body with the touch of her lips on mine.

"I'm glad you're early."

"I thought I could help you pack. Mother's insisted that you two stay at our place tomorrow night if it looks dodgy." I smiled up at her. "Hey, I had nothing to do with it. Cross my heart."

"I —" I froze. What had I almost said? It felt so natural, so right to be in her arms, that I had almost said *I love you*. I bit my lower lip really hard and winced at the pain.

"What? What's wrong?" I forced a laugh and kissed her.

"Nothing. Come upstairs for a few minutes. Mel," I called as we went past, "Jenn's here. We're going to be in the loft."

"Right. Ignore all sounds from here on out," Melissa responded from the bedroom with a giggle.

We climbed the stairs, and I pulled Jenn down onto me as I lay back across the bed. She rested on her elbows and looked down at me. "Want to tell me what's really wrong?"

"I don't want to lose this place," I said helplessly. "And there isn't a damn thing I can do about it." She bent to kiss my forehead.

"Maybe old Anatoli will turn out to sea."

"And maybe he'll decide to come crashing ashore right here. I'm ... I'm scared, Jenn. I don't know why, but I am. Christ, I've lived through a dozen hurricanes; I used to think they were really cool. But now it's my house that's going to go floating out to sea with all the lamps still burning, and I'm scared half to death."

"Hush. Everything will be fine, just so long as you stay safe." I reached up for her and pulled her down against me, wanting her comfort and her support in a way I hadn't wanted anyone's since my mother died.

"Hold me. Just hold me until we have to go downstairs."

"I will, darling. I will."

* * *

The Millikans arrived promptly at seven. Jenn and I had just come back downstairs, and Jenn was playing bartender while I greeted the guests. Belinda had called Mel, so she was hiding in the bedroom talking on the phone.

"Oh, my, it looks so empty without all those pictures. Your mother was such a photographer," Janie Millikan said. I looked around at the bare walls.

"Yes. They had to come down at the end of the summer anyway, so better safe than sorry."

"Really rotten about this storm, Katie," Roger Millikan told me in his gruff tone. "Really rotten. Told your dad years ago he should build a sea wall, but he didn't listen. Said the beach would go back the other way any time, and there'd be no problem." I had no reply for this, so I turned to Angela.

"You picked a good time to leave." I smiled. Angela and I have known each other since we were small children. She's two years older than I am, twice divorced, with two children in their early teens. She taught history at UNC-Greensboro and lived, last she'd written me which was the annual Christmas card exchange, that she was sharing a house with a fellow professor of unmentioned sex.

"Well, Frank insists that I get back before the summer term starts." I nodded as if this made perfect sense to me, and offered her a drink. Roger was trying to bully aside Jenn by telling her good-naturedly that she didn't know how to mix a Bloody Mary the way he liked it. I opened a soda and Angela had one too, and we all went out on the front deck to watch the whitecaps.

I stood between Angela and Jenn, and realized that this might be the last time I would look out on the Atlantic from this particular location. It was a searing thought. The tide was higher than usual, as the storm approached it would get higher, and the waves were breaking to within feet of our stairs.

"The sea is wild tonight," Jenn murmured. "Like a wounded heart. It beats itself upon the shore with useless remorse." I glanced at her curiously. She met my eyes with a gaze that told me she meant something I might not want to know.

"How very literary," Angela commented. "Have you taken up poetry, Jennifer?" Jenn smiled a little and shook her head, no. "Well, you should."

"I was going to grill steaks outside," I said aloud. "But I think we'll have to settle for the Jenn-Air in the kitchen."

"That's fine with us, dear," Janie said. She and Roger were standing together a few steps from Angela, looking out over the waves with an awe not unlike our own. Something about a stormy sea affects all people alike. It hypnotizes them.

Melissa joined us on the deck, slipping between me and Angela. She put a hand on my back quickly, then let it drop, a silent gesture of strength. "Belinda said hi."

"Oh. How's the house?"

"Still standing. I mean ...." We looked at each other, but I've known Melissa too long to fault her lack of tact. "They've finished the roof."

"Good. Well, shall we wander inside where it isn't quite so nippy?" I had started a fire in the woodstove, and as everyone else stood around it to warm their hands, I went to the kitchen to start dinner. Angela followed me, though I didn't know it was her at first and thought it was Jenn.

"How are you holding up?" Her voice was concerned.

"I'll live."

"Can I say something that might sound very strange to you?"

"Sure, Angela. Anything." She cleared her throat.

"It might be better if this house goes into the sea. I've sensed something not right about it ever since the summer Caroline died."

I stared at her, my jaw hanging slack.

"I know, that sounds really weird. But sometimes, when people die unexpectedly, their souls get – tied to an earthly place...."

"Ghosts. You sense Caroline's ghost in this house?" Angela nodded. I went pale. The bar was three steps through the archway and I was there in two, pouring myself a straight bourbon. Angela's face was a mask of concern as I rejoined her, pulling her by the arm farther away from the open pass through to the living room.

"What are you doing, Katherine? I thought you stopped drinking." I took a long, burning swallow and nodded.

"I did. Tell me about this – this presence."

"Just that. It's unhappy. If Caroline died in the sea, and her ghost is tied to this house because of it, then sending this house to the sea is the way to release her spirit."

"Why would she be tied to this house?" I wanted to know what Angela knew, what she was guessing, and what she thought she was talking about. I took another swallow.

"Oh, come on, Katherine. She was in love with you. This was the closest thing that had a part of you in it. Where else would she go?" Angela's expression told me to stop acting foolishly.

"How do you know she was in love with me?"

If she mentions that lighthouse, I'm going to scream.

"The same way I know you were in love with her. I'm not an idiot, Kate. I was in your apartment in Chapel Hill enough to know what was going on."

"Oh." I wondered who else knew and had never said anything to me about it. "Angela, I think I've seen her."

"What?" I explained about the two times I had seen Caroline going into the water. Angela nodded as if this proved her point, which I rather thought it did. "You see what I mean?"

"Yes, I think I do." At that point, Jenn came in to see why I was hiding in the kitchen.

"Okay, what're you two up to?" Angela held up her hands.

"I didn't touch her, I swear. Frank'd kill me."

Jenn stared at her. Then she turned and gave me a look of pure anger. Angela intercepted it and waved a time-out.

"I was joking. Jeez, don't be so homophobic." Slowly, Jenn relaxed, but I had seen the look in her eyes. I hadn't realized how deeply in the closet she was until that moment. It frightened me a little bit.

"Are you about ready to put the steaks on?" I nodded dumbly. "Good. I'll get the salad out then." She went to the refrigerator. I followed her out to the dining table, then touched her elbow.

"Could I speak to you for a moment?" I led her into the spare bedroom and closed the door, then turned an angry face to her. "What the Hell was that? Do you really think I'd out you?"

"I didn't know. I'm sorry. My parents having their own suspicions is one thing, they'll leave me alone. But if they hear a rumor ...." She paced a few feet. "It's easy for you."

"You had no right to look at me like that in front of one of my guests!" She dropped her head.

"I'm sorry. I – I guess I was jealous." That took me aback.

"Jealous? Why?"

"I don't know. It was stupid. I didn't come in there to cause a scene, I ... just when I saw you with that drink ... I didn't know what to think." I looked down at the bourbon. It was half gone.

"We were talking about Caroline. Angela said she's felt a presence in the house. I told her I'd seen Caroline's ghost."

"You what?" Jenn laughed, sobering quickly when she realized I was serious. "When?" I told her. She crossed her arms and looked concerned.

"I thought I was just imagining things."

"Great. You tell me that the ghost of your one true love is hanging around this place, and we've been having sex here for a week?" We stared at each other, and then I started to giggle. I was a little tipsy, but when she put it that way, it sounded ridiculous. After a moment, Jenn joined me.

"Don't worry, Caroline was never a voyeur," I managed. Jenn grinned and caught me in a hug. We kissed briefly, then went back out to the living room. I apologized for the delay in dinner, then returned to the kitchen to put the steaks on the Jenn-Air grill.

*   *   *

The Millikans left just after ten. Mel, Jenn and I sat around and listened to the weather forecast on the radio, and plotted Anatoli's course as he headed straight for us. Outside, it had started to rain lightly. I threw another log into the wood stove and came back to the couch, snuggling up close to Jenn. The bourbon had gone straight to my head, and I was feeling slightly fuzzy still, though by no means drunk.

Mel went to bed at ten thirty, leaving the two of us curled up together in the living room. After her door had closed, Jenn looked down and kissed me on the forehead.

"It'll be okay," she said softly. I lay my head on her shoulder.

"I wish I could believe you."

"I wish I could make Anatoli turn around." I smiled into her neck and kissed her throat. She murmured something.

"Jenn ...." I looked up at her.

"Yes, darling?"

- 120 -

"Stay with me tonight." She pushed me gently away and stared at me. "I don't want to be alone. Not tonight."

"Kat, are you sure?" I nodded. "Yes. I'll stay. I'll have to call my parents, but they'll understand." I watched her walk to the kitchen and make the call. She was on the phone but a minute, then returned to the couch and held out her hands.

"That was quick," I said. She nodded.

"I told dad that you had asked me to stay up with you in case things got bad. He thought me admirable for agreeing." I smiled and took her hands. She led me upstairs, then sat on the edge of the bed quietly, folding her hands in her lap.

"What are you doing?"

"I'm waiting for you to tell me what you want me to do."

I was surprised. "I figured you'd already have my clothes half off."

"Is that what you want?" I considered her question. What I wanted was to feel the kind of warm comfort you can only get from drifting off into a quiet sleep after making love with someone you care very deeply for.

"No." I sat astride her lap, gently running my fingers down her jaw. "What I want ... " I unbuttoned her blouse slowly, taking my time with each button. " ... is to ... " I reached behind her and unfastened her bra and slid both shirt and bra down off her arms. Her nipples lay soft, hardening as I cupped her breasts and caressed them. " ... make slow," My mouth bent to her throat to kiss her. "gentle," My lips worked down toward the curve of her chest. "love ... " She groaned as I ran a light tongue across one of her nipples. " ... until we ... " I tasted the other nipple, then returned to the first. " ... fall asleep ... " I reached for her belt, unbuckling it with the same slow care. " ... in each other's arms." I unzipped her slacks and slipped them down over her hips, along with her underwear, and at the same time fastened my mouth to her breast and applied my weight to press her back across the bed.

I caressed her, teased her with my fingers, as she pleaded with me in a hoarse whisper to take her. I wet my fingers with her moisture, then brought up my hand and ran it around each nipple, bending my head to take it between my teeth just after, tasting her and flicking at the hardness with my tongue. Jenn groaned unintelligibly, running her fingers through my hair, trying to push my head down her body toward her silken blonde mound, lifting her hips to try and capture my hand and pull it inside her. I danced away from that hungry, warm well, spreading her lips with my fingers, caressing her clitoris as I moved across her, suckling at her breasts like a newborn babe.

Her movements became more and more erratic, and I knew that I had taken her to the pinnacle of arousal, that one movement would send her into a thousand spasms of pleasure. I moved between her legs, spread them slightly, and pressed my hand in with a sudden thrust, filling her. Her back arched and she cried out with the sudden stillness, once only, then splintered into a violent orgasm that shook her body.

Then it was over and I was beside her, kissing her dry lips tenderly, still fully clothed. She lay still for a time, then folded me in her arms and began my seduction.

X.

I woke the next morning with my face buried in Jenn's hair. I took a deep breath, smelling the scent of her shampoo, then rolled over and opened my eyes to the day.

It was raining fiercely, and I thought I felt a constant trembling through the house. For a terrible moment, I had the vision that we had been swept out to sea during the night, and were floating somewhere in the Atlantic Ocean in the middle of a tropical storm, waiting to die.

I crawled out of the bed. Jenn rolled over into the warm space I had left and pulled the blankets up around her head. I pulled on my nightshirt and, crossing to the balcony doors, opened one and stepped outside. Ignoring the driving rain, I went to the railing and looked over. Waves broke to within a yard of the bottom steps of the house, but we were still firmly rooted in terra firma. The shaking I felt came from the pounding of the surf so close to the foundation.

Relief flooded my mind, and I slipped back inside and closed the door, leaning against it with my wet back. I looked across the room at the bed where Jenn still slept, oblivious to the fact that I was gone. I imagined she was one of those people for whom mornings were a daily torture. There, at least, she was different from Caroline, who used to go jogging every morning at around six AM.

I considered crawling back into bed and waking Jenn up, but as I walked toward her, she rolled onto her side and sighed in her sleep. I looked down at a face so sweetly innocent that I didn't have the heart to wake her, so I got my clothes and slipped downstairs.

In the shower, I recalled how she had made love to me the night before, the feel of her fingers and lips on me, the way her hair fell across my face as we kissed. After a long time, during which we mostly held and kissed one another, I had drifted off into exactly the sort of sleep I was hoping for. I realized now, as I stepped out of the shower and reached for a towel, that I hadn't even taken my sleeping pill; the first night I'd been able to sleep without it in years.

I pulled on jeans and a sweatshirt and wandered out into the kitchen, pouring a cup of day old coffee and putting it in the microwave. As I waited for it to heat, I turned on the radio in the kitchen and tuned it to the public radio station out of UNC-Wilmington. Jazz filled the air.

As I was putting creamer in my coffee, Melissa came out of her room, yawning and stretching. "Good morning," I said.

"Morning," she returned. "Heard the weather yet?"

I shook my head. "Jenn's still asleep."

"You probably wore her out." I shook my head again. My body felt so warm and wonderful, not even the impending doom of my beloved house could make me feel totally depressed.

"I doubt it." The selection ended and the announcer came on with the weather forecast. When I heard it, I almost couldn't believe my ears. I had to go and chart the coordinates to make sure I wasn't hearing things. During the night, Anatoli had turned east, and was bearing along the coast on a northeasterly line. It was expected to just brush us, with a storm surge of only a foot. I stared at my chart and slowly sank onto the couch.

"Katherine?" Melissa came out to join me. I pointed to the chart. "It's going to miss us?"

"Not entirely. But we can survive a one-foot surge. The garage'll get a little wet, but I don't think the house is going to collapse." Mel leaned over and gave me a quick hug.

"I'm glad." I ran a hand through my still wet hair and looked around, a wave of relief running through me. It was hard to believe how upset I'd been at the thought of losing the place. I wondered how hard it would be to put up that sea wall Roger Millikan had been talking about.

"I'm going to take some breakfast up to Jenn," I told Melissa. "I think this calls for breakfast in bed, don't you?" She nodded. I went into the kitchen and fixed up a quick breakfast of bagels, bacon, scrambled eggs and fresh coffee, put it on a tray, and went upstairs with it.

Jenn was still on her side, the covers tucked up under her chin. Her hair was falling half-over her face, and I was struck with a strange sense of comfortable pleasure as I looked down at her. I could get used to seeing her like this. Sighing, I put down the tray and sat down beside her on the bed.

She mumbled something when I touched her shoulder, and flipped onto her back. Smiling gently, I leaned over and kissed her lips. She came awake all at once, her mouth opening to mine.

"Good morning, darling," I whispered, brushing her hair out of her eyes. She smiled up at me.

"Good morning."

"I brought breakfast." I reached for the tray and sat it on the bed between us. Jenn's eyes sparkled. "Anatoli decided he didn't want to fight a bunch of dykes."

"The storm turned? Oh, Kat, that's wonderful!" Her arms went around me in a tight hug. I returned it, glad for the warmth of her body, and offered her a plate of food.

"After last night, I figured I'd better treat you right," I teased. "Since your parents were so accommodating to let you sleep over. I wouldn't want them to think I'd taken advantage of you."

"Oh, you didn't," she replied, grinning as she reached for a bagel. "But I won't turn down this kind of pampering."

I sipped at my coffee and watched her eating. Now that the threat had passed, I could see the romantic aspects of our setting; the rain outside, the two of us together in the loft, breakfast and coffee in bed. If Melissa hadn't been sitting downstairs, I would probably have given Jenn something special for dessert. But I didn't want to be quiet.

For her size, Jenn is a dainty eater. She took small bites and chewed everything thoroughly. I've always just sort of piled food in and swallowed. But Jenn made it look like an art form. I watched her cut her pile of eggs into ten equal sections, taking a bite of bacon after each section had been eaten. If she noticed that I was staring at her, she didn't say anything.

"So are you going to ride the storm out here?" She asked finally, taking her coffee. I shook my head.

"After I board up the windows, I'm outta here. There'll be water under the house, and I'm not so sure I want to be that close to the ocean. I thought I'd avail myself of your mother's hospitality."

"Well, you're both welcome. We can play pinochle or cribbage or something. Anything but bridge." I laughed. My mother had been an avid bridge player, and I knew exactly how Jenn felt.

"Don't worry. How did you sleep?"

"Pretty well. You know, you move around a lot. I don't think you're used to sleeping with someone." I blushed.

"I'm not. I haven't had a live-in lover since ...." I didn't finish the sentence, and neither did Jenn. After a pause, I continued. "I've got a queen sized bed at home, and I'm used to just spreading out over it."

"I can tell." I studied her face for a moment, then let my eyes drop to her bare chest. She was sitting there in bed as though we woke up together every morning. It was all so domestic, so nice. I felt a pain in my heart.

"Jenn ...." She looked at me. "I – you'd better get dressed or I'm going to ravish you." I was comfortable on a sexual level. Sex without intimacy has been my trademark for many years.

The intimacy I was beginning to feel for Jenn scared me. I reacted by trying to hold the relationship at arm's length, trying to act as though her body was all that I was interested in, although looking at her was stirring me to desire.

"Ravish away," she responded, leaning back against the wall. "I like being ravished by you."

I carefully removed the tray containing the breakfast dishes to the bedside table, and turned back to her. Sliding my hands up the sides of her ribcage, I leaned in and kissed her.

"Why do you have to be so damn willing?" I muttered as I pulled her down, having shed my own clothes in an untidy pile on the floor. She wrapped her legs around me and smiled through our kiss.

"Why do you have to be so damn good?"

*   *   *

Monday morning, I met the insurance adjuster at the ferry. We drove to the house, and he surveyed the damage, three broken front windows, all the sheet rock in the front room soaking wet, the front steps torn away and the sand seriously eroded from around the front posts of the deck. Inside, there was a thick layer of sand and broken glass across the wet carpet, and much of the living room furniture was overturned and soaked.

The paperwork was filled out and the adjuster went on to another client whose house had suffered slightly less damage than mine. His final words echoed in my head as I drove back to the Brooks'. *You understand that without any seaward protection, we can't continue your coverage ....* I went straight to the telephone upon arriving at Jenn's and called Roger Millikan for the name of a company that would move the house and build a sea wall.

By Monday afternoon I had someone out from the Owner's Association surveying the lot to determine how far back I could have the house moved. We argued back and forth, and finally agreed that I could set the house back another twenty-eight feet, enough to build up artificial dunes and put in a retaining wall.

Tuesday, over protestations from Mrs. Brooks, I rented a villa and Melissa and I moved ourselves there. The furniture from the living room was removed and sent to the mainland for cleaning, and the carpet ripped up. Wednesday, a crew started repairing the house. By Thursday, when Melissa was preparing to return to Seattle, half the island had heard about what I was doing.

I had expected it to be a massive undertaking to move a house. To my surprise, I was told that although the work couldn't be started until September, it would only take a week to actually accomplish the feat. The difficult part would be the construction of the sea wall and dunes.

Jenn and I drove Melissa to the Wilmington airport on Friday. She was taking a commuter plane to Raleigh, and from there had a non-stop Delta flight home. Belinda was meeting her in Seattle, and I could tell that Mel was more than anxious to see her again. I was a little anxious, too. With Melissa gone, I would have the house to myself for the rest of the summer. That meant I didn't have to work around her in order to have Jenn over.

Jenn and I had hardly had any time alone all week. I had been so busy with all the necessary arrangements for repairing the house that I'd been unable to do much of anything else, except stare at my computer and try to concentrate on work. By Friday afternoon, I was ready to tear my hair out. Jenn stopped by as I was trying to concentrate on the closing market statistics on the television. She rapped on the door, then came in.

"Am I interrupting?" I looked up, and felt a surge of relief.

"Not at all." I rose and met her halfway across the living room, holding out my arms. She stepped into them and kissed me firmly. "I was hoping you'd come back over today."

"Are you kidding? When you finally have a place all to yourself?" She kissed me again. I wanted to melt into her arms and stay there forever.

"Can you stay for a while?" Jenn made an affirmative sound, her lips working across my neck toward my shoulder. "Oh, sweetheart, you don't know what you're doing to me ...."

"Yes, I do," she replied, grinning at me. "I'm giving you a commendation for your work all week. Starting with a long, slow massage ...." I allowed her start pushing me toward the bedroom door.

* * *

"How long are you planning to stay?" I asked some time later. Jenn rolled over and looked at the dim light outside the window. The sun had set almost an hour before, and the last light was just fading.

"Oh, I don't know. All night?" I sat up, the sheet falling away from my bare chest.

"All night?" I echoed. "What about your parents?"

Jenn shrugged, then smiled at me. "They've gone home for the weekend. Some medical dinner they had to go to." I laughed and reached over to tickle her just under the short ribs.

"You little ... when were you going to tell me you had all weekend free?"

"I just did. Now, get back here." I snuggled back into the pillows and felt her arms around me. "I hope you don't mind me asking to stay here while they're gone ... I'm scared to be alone." She was using a little girl's voice that made me giggle.

"Of course not. I wouldn't want the boogieman to get you. In fact, to make sure you're safe, I think I'll keep you right here." We kissed again, deeply.

Saturday morning dawned a brilliant blue, the sun peeking through the half-drawn shades of the bedroom to awaken me from a deep, full sleep. I fought against opening my eyes for a few minutes, lulled by the warmth of Jenn's body next to mine, her arm across my chest, her face nestled against my shoulder.

I finally came fully awake and lay there, feeling her breath on my neck. I stared at the ceiling, not wanting to move, not wanting the moment to end. Then, in response to something in a dream perhaps, Jenn shifted and rolled over onto her side with her back to me. I slipped my legs over the side of the bed and stood up, reaching for my robe.

The villa was much smaller than the house, and it was only a few short steps into the kitchen, where I started a pot of coffee and pulled out the cereal for breakfast. I turned the television on, muted the volume, and watched a cartoon I hadn't seen in years on Nickelodeon.

In the years since I started dating again, I've had women stay at my house on numerous occasions. But I don't encourage it. If a relationship lasts six months, I would guess my lover would have slept over at my place no more than ten times. I only let women sleep over at all on the weekends, and I preferred that it not become a habit. In fact, when it started to happen twice a week, when I found that maybe once I might want to have someone stay over on a weeknight, I took it as a sign that I needed to get away from that particular person, that it was becoming too real.

Three times in those years, I've had a woman accompany me on vacation. All three times, I felt uncomfortable waking up next to my lover day after day. But with Jenn, I felt so relaxed and rested that it was hard to imagine not wanting to have her there. I stared at the television and wondered when I would start to run away. It's never a conscious decision that I make; I don't wake up one morning and tell myself that this is the day I'm going to throw a screaming bitch fit because my lover does something minor and gives me an excuse to.

The coffee finished brewing and I got myself a cup. Fixing it, I took it out onto the deck and looked out across the golf course toward the lighthouse. The villa I was in didn't face the sea, which was the reason I'd been able to get into it on such short notice. But it had a decent view of the eighteenth fairway, so I wasn't going to complain. The workmen had assured me I would be able to return to my house by the coming Friday.

If this had been a normal morning, if I had been in Seattle and the woman asleep in my bed had been anyone but Jenn, I would have fixed a tray and taken coffee in to her, offered to start a shower for her, and taken her clothes downstairs to iron. I pamper my lovers; right up until I actually start to feel intimate with them. Then I turn stone cold.

As it was, I had no great desire to go in and wake Jenn up. She had looked very comfortable when I'd left the room, and I wanted to let her sleep. It was as if we'd been sleeping together for years. I was taking my morning breather before we spent the day together.

I sat and sipped my coffee, and remembered how she had made love to me the night before, how she had held me and stroked me with tender hands, then turned fierce and wanton within the space of a breath, taking me to heights of passion I thought I could no longer reach. And I returned her pleasure, bringing her to climax after climax. I wondered idly what time we had fallen asleep finally.

Remembering stirred me, and I found myself going back inside, setting my coffee mug on the kitchen counter, and walking quietly into the bedroom. Jenn was still asleep, now on her stomach, her arms wrapped around a pillow. The sheets were falling off of her legs, the only part of her still covered, and

I stood at the end of the bed and looked down at the length of her naked back, her smooth round buttocks. Her hair fell across her face.

I slowly unfastened my robe, slid it off, and pulled the sheet completely off of her. Then I gently knelt beside her and began to kiss along her spine, from her shoulders down. She stirred, and started to move.

"Stay still," I whispered sternly. Her movement ceased, and I continued down her back until I reached the small hollow at the base of her spine. Then I put my hands out and spread her legs enough to allow me to move between them, kissing along the curve of her hips, my hands now caressing her thighs, dipping down to trace across her moistness.

"Oh, Kat ...." Jenn moaned, burying her face in the pillow. "Stop teasing me ...." I slipped inside her, felt her tighten against me, then open again in a wet flood. I began to move within her, my fingers and the sides of my knees the only parts of my body touching hers. She groaned loudly and pressed against the mattress, setting a rhythm for me to follow.

I leaned forward, cupping my hand to the shape of her body as I took her more forcefully. She gave herself to me, opening fully to my questing, thrusting fingers. I brought her to orgasm, kept within her until she had stopped spasming, then withdrew and lay the length of my body down on hers, my chest pressing into her shoulder blades.

"Good morning, darling," I said softly, kissing her cheek through the tangle of hair, gently rotating my own wet mound against the softness of her buttocks. She started to turn underneath me, but I stopped her, my hands pinning her shoulders to the bed. I brought my legs up to straddle her waist and began to rock against her, pressing down onto her. It took a matter of scant minutes before I gathered into sudden stillness, unable to breathe, back arched for a long silent moment.

Then I allowed her to roll me over so that she was between my legs, looking down into my face. "Katherine, I swear ...."

"You don't like to be woke up that way?" I asked innocently, batting my eyelids at her. She growled deep in her throat and bent her head to kiss me on the mouth.

"I'll show you how much I don't like it," she replied, her hands on my hips. She flexed her arm muscles and lifted me, at the same time pulling her legs up under her so that she crouched back on her heels with her thighs under my buttocks. The arching of my back sent darts of pleasure through my nipples, and a fresh wave of warm moisture to my groin.

Jenn's fingers sought out my clitoris, then with her thumb pressed firmly against it she delved within me with her middle and forefingers, taking me. I wrapped my legs around her waist and came again, almost instantly, unable to withstand the intense pleasure. I cried her name, clawing at the sheets with fists that spasmed in time with my body.

Then she was beside me, holding me to her chest, rocking me softly, kissing me so tenderly that I almost couldn't feel her lips. Until her tongue reached out and touched mine with an electric jolt. I wanted her, wanted to taste her. I tried to pull her up to straddle my face, but she pulled away, turning around so that we lay side by side, my head to the top of the bed, hers to the bottom. She put her arms around my waist and rolled over, pulling me on top of her.

"Together," she said simply. Then there was only sweet, wet pleasure.

*　　*　　*

We played tennis that morning then packed a picnic lunch and rode up to east beach where we hunted shells and made love in the dunes. That evening, I asked her to accompany me to dinner at the club dining room. She agreed, and went home to dress. I took great care in choosing my ensemble; I wanted to look good escorting her to dinner. I chose a long black cotton skirt with a slit up the side, a white blouse with a frill, and a long black linen double-breasted jacket. I slipped my feet into my black pumps, styled my hair, applied makeup for the third time that trip, and carefully put on the strand of pearls my mother had left me.

I call this my power-lunch outfit. The clothes are all custom tailored, and I usually wear it when I have to go downtown to lunch with Jean or one of my bankers. I had only packed it on the trip because it was the closest thing I own to a formal, other than the set of tails in my closet in Seattle, and I don't think that would go over very well at Smith Island.

Jenn was to meet me back at the villa, from whence we would drive to the club. I could actually see the clubhouse from the deck, at the end of the eighteenth hole. I mixed a cranberry spritzer and sat down to wait for her.

She arrived on time, and when I opened the door for her, I had to stop momentarily and catch my breath. I'd never seen her in a dress. The one she wore was of cream linen, a simple, classic cut that tapered at her calves and was accented with a wide belt braided of multi-colored cords at her waist. The neckline took a daring plunge down the front, revealing enough of her cleavage to make me sweat. She had on matching pumps, and a single gold necklace with a cloisonné pendant. Her hair was curled and loose, falling in soft waves around her face.

"Oh, my." It was all I could manage. I stepped back and allowed her in. She looked me up and down and grinned the familiar grin that reminded me I was not looking at a model. I had thought her striking before, now she was downright beautiful.

"You look fabulous," Jenn said, stepping in to kiss me. I caught a whiff of perfume on her, not her usual Polo. I thought it might be Chanel, but I wasn't certain.

"So do you." We stared at each other for a while longer.

"We have reservations," she finally reminded me. I looked down at my watch and nodded.

"Yes." I got my keys and followed her outside. As I walked down the stairs behind her, I couldn't help but notice the smoothness of her dress where it crossed her hips. Neither of us was wearing hose, as our legs had become tanned from exposure to the summer sun. As I helped her into the golf cart I asked casually, "Are you wearing anything under that?"

She laughed and gave me The Smile. "Not a thing."

I was instantly soaked, and blushing furiously. "Oh."

"Something for you to think about during dinner, darling."

Somehow, I managed to get us there without wrecking.

After dinner, I drove over to the public beach access by my house and parked. Kicking off my shoes, I helped Jenn out and we walked to the beach, barefoot, hand in hand. Strolling along the edge of the water, my head against her shoulder, her arm around my waist, I looked up the shoreline and wondered how I could possibly feel so happy.

"Do you remember the first walk we took together?" Jenn asked, looking over at me with a faint smile.

"Yes. I wanted you even then. Even though I kept remembering how you used to torment Lynne and me when you were thirteen."

She laughed softly. "And I thought you were taken already. I'm glad you weren't."

Despite the warning bell that went off in my head, I snuggled closer to her and smiled.

"I've been very happy since I've been here."

"I'm glad." We walked along in silence, feeling one another's presence. I found, as we turned back the way we had come, that I didn't want it to end. Not just the walk, the summer. Us.

We kissed briefly before leaving the beach, and as my hands went to her hips I was reminded again what she had said she was wearing under her dress. Suddenly, I wanted to get her back to the villa as quickly as possible.

XI.

The sun was warm on my back, and the glass of champagne cool against my hand. I raised up to take a sip, glancing over at the ice chest to make sure it was closed against the heat. Caroline was looking back at me, naked from the waist up, the top of her bathing suit laying beside her on the towel.

"Someone's going to come by and see those tits pointing to the sky," I told her, reaching over with the hand that held the champagne to pour a little over one soft breast. She shivered and pushed at my hand.

"Quit it! What do you think you're doing?"

"Teasing you," I replied, moving toward her. We were both just a little drunk, a little careless about our actions. She groaned when I leaned over and lapped at the sticky champagne on her skin, my tongue crossing her nipple.

"Christ, mon ami ...." Caroline lapsed into French. It was her minor, something to complement her music major. I loved it when she spoke to me in that Gallic language while I made love to her. She could have been quoting the price of pigs feet for all I knew, but the sound of the words spilling from her lips drove me wild.

I fastened my mouth to her swelling breast, suckling at her mindless of the exposure of our position on the beach. There wasn't anyone else around, and there wasn't likely to be. Ours was the only house for a mile, and since the inlanders had to make use of public beach access points, the closest of which was half a mile away, I wasn't expecting company.

She pushed me away suddenly and sat up, reaching for her bikini top. I rolled over onto my knees, watching as she put it on. "What's wrong, C?"

"It's hot. I want to go swimming. Come on." I groaned and looked out at the water. It was inviting, almost glass smooth in the windless sun. But the idea of swimming with half a bottle of champagne in me didn't sound appealing.

"Naw, you go ahead. I'll just watch." She tossed her head.

"Spoil sport. Okay, you just watch." She stood and brushed sand from her legs, then picked her way down to the edge of the water. Caroline was fearless in water. I watched her wade out past the small breakers until she was hip deep, then with a powerful dive she went underwater. I watched as she resurfaced quite a way away, her dark wet hair falling down her back. She looked like a mermaid.

Caroline was an expert swimmer. She had been on the UNC junior varsity women's swim team for a year, and I had no worries that she could handle herself.

The sun was making me drowsy, so I drained my glass and set it aside, then opened the ice chest for an apple. Our vacation was drawing to a close. My parents would be down the next week, and two weeks after that it would be time to return to Chapel Hill and take up the books for our final year. I couldn't wait, and had already begun poring over grad catalogs trying to decide where I wanted to take my masters.

Caroline said it didn't matter where we lived, as long as we were together. I could wholeheartedly agree with her on that.

Down the beach, I saw a group of people walking along the shoreline together. They bent now and again, probably looking at shells. It would take them ten or fifteen minutes to reach me. I grinned to myself. If Caroline hadn't gone swimming, we might have given them something really interesting to look at. I took a bite of my apple.

Sitting back, I looked out over the water. I didn't see Caroline immediately. She was probably underwater again. She loved to hold her breath and swim underwater. I had watched her in the pool, making strong strokes from one end to the other without breaking the surface for air. I continued to watch. She still didn't surface.

Long seconds passed. I began to grow concerned. Dropping the apple, I got to my feet and put my hand up to shield my eyes as I scanned the sea. Nothing. A knot of fear took hold of my stomach, twisting it. Then she came up all at once, as if she had pushed off from the bottom with a mighty kick. I started to call to her, but she came back down into the water, face first. She wasn't moving.

I could hear the hammering of my heart as I started running toward the water. From somewhere I heard the high wail of seagulls, only to realize that it was my voice, screaming her name. I hit the water in a dead run, got to my calves, and fell. Spitting sand and water, I scrambled back to my feet and continued toward where Caroline lay so still.

She was so far out and I wasn't a strong swimmer. I felt the sea pulling at me as I struggled out to her, trying to force me back to land. It seemed like forever before I was even out far enough to start swimming, then I struck out with all my might. I got to her, finally, and rolled her over. Her head lolled back.

I slipped an arm around her chest and held her to me as I started back in, trying to remember the lifesaving stroke she herself had taught me. I was panicked, choking water as I fought to keep our heads above the surface. I saw the people on the beach running toward me, found bottom with my feet and picked Caroline up in my arms.

She was like a rag doll. Tears streaming down my face, I stumbled out onto the beach, up past the running waves, and collapsed, dropping her to the sand. I tried to remember my CPR class. Mechanically, I started trying to resuscitate her.

There were people around me suddenly, people asking questions, a man in brightly flowered swimming trunks claiming to be a doctor kneeling over Caroline, and I was screaming, fighting to be back beside her, struggling against the hands that held me. An ambulance came tearing up the beach, siren wailing. And through it all Caroline lay there, motionless.

She lied! She lied, she's gone and left me and she swore she never would .... Oh, Caroline, how can I live without you .... Don't do this to me .... God! Caroline!

* * *

"Katherine!"

Someone shook me. I woke with Jenn's strong hands on my arms. She shook me again. In the light of the bedside lamp, her face was white with concern.

"Katherine! Look at me!" I blinked at her through my tears, trying to clear my head. *Jenny Brooks is only thirteen, she couldn't possibly be this strong ....* "Katherine, you're scaring me. Stop screaming!"

"Jenny ... Jenn?" I came back to the present, to the villa, to the two of us naked together in the bed. It wasn't 1984. It was 1999, and I wasn't twenty and Jenn wasn't thirteen, and Caroline was dead, and had been dead for fifteen years.

"Goddess, Katherine, I was so frightened .... You wouldn't wake up!" Jenn enfolded me in her arms. I felt tense, uncomfortable. Jenn sensed this and let go of me. "Kat?"

"I ...." I had to get out of the bedroom. Throwing back the cover, I rolled out of bed and dashed out into the kitchen, grabbing my robe on the way. It was three fifteen in the morning, and the sky was black. I stood in the darkened kitchen, shaking uncontrollably. It had been so vivid, everything exactly as it had happened. Like it had been at first, those first years. I had forgotten just how terrifying and nauseating the dream was.

"Katherine," Jenn's voice from the doorway was quiet, flat. I put my hands on the counter to steady them, and dropped my head. I couldn't face her, not after this. Melissa had told me that I often called for Caroline in my sleep, and if I had been screaming, what had I said? I heard footsteps behind me. "Kat, are you going to be all right?"

"In the bathroom, by the sink ... there's a vial marked Atavan. Bring it to me." My heart wouldn't stop pounding, trying to break from my chest. I was having an anxiety attack. I fought for breath, clenched my fists and wanted to beat them against the counter until they were bloody. I've had a prescription for anti-anxiety medication ever since I was released from the hospital following Caroline's death. I hadn't taken one of the pills in months, but I needed it now.

Jenn returned with the bottle, and I fumbled the cap open and took out the pill, took it dry, then drank from the tap to wash it down. It would take about five minutes to work. I should have taken my sleeping pill. Forcing myself to stop shaking, I switched on the kitchen light and turned to face Jenn.

"I'm having a panic attack," I explained, unable to find words to explain what had happened. Jenn's eyes were wide, and she nodded dumbly. I looked down, saw that my fingernails were digging into my palms, and opened my fists. "I'll be okay in a minute. Just give me a minute ...."

"Kat – " She took a step forward, lifting her arms.

"No. Don't touch me." She stopped and looked hurt. "I'm sorry, Jenn." I wanted her to hold me, but I was afraid to let her, afraid that it would be too much.

"I only wanted ...."

"I know." *I know, darling. Sweet, wonderful, caring Jenn ....*

I felt the calming begin. Sighing deeply, I welcomed it. Jenn watched me from under her eyelids, leaning against the refrigerator with her arms crossed in front of her.

"It was about Caroline, wasn't it."

"Don't say her name. I can't bear it." I felt sick for a moment. Almost as an afterthought, I added, "Yes."

Jenn was silent, chewing on her upper lip.

"Do you want to talk about it?" She asked finally.

"There's no point," I replied. "It won't go away."

"I'd like to know." She shifted tentatively. "It's a part of you. I accept that. But I'd like to know more about it. Do you dream a lot?" I smiled ruefully and nodded.

"It comes and goes. Since I've been here, it's been pretty bad... but this has been the worst."

"Is there anything I can do?" She looked earnest.

"Jenn, I ... I warned you I wasn't someone you wanted to get involved with. This is just the tip of the iceberg."

She shrugged. "And I told you I wanted to make that decision. Just tell me what you need from me."

"I'm not sure," I said truthfully. "Right now I just want to be alone. In five minutes I might want to be held."

"Okay. Kat, it's okay to be scared. It's okay to be upset. It's also okay to need someone. Don't think you have to be strong all the time. It doesn't work forever."

"Thanks. Go back to bed, Jenn. I'll be there in a while." She turned and went back into the bedroom. I stood in the kitchen for a while longer, staring out the window into the darkness, then flipped the light off and returned to bed.

Jenn was on her side, facing away from me. When I slipped in beside her, she rolled over and looked at me. I could just make out her eyes. "Will you be able to sleep?"

"Yes, darling. Thanks for understanding." I allowed her to take me in her arms and pressed my face into her chest. But long after her breathing had slowed into sleep, I stayed awake, feeling her body next to me.

* * *

I woke Sunday morning to an empty bed. Startled, I looked around the room; Jenn's clothes were gone. I fell back into the pillows, stunned. She'd left. After the night before I thought I shouldn't be surprised, but I was. I'd had more than one woman decide she couldn't deal with the memory of a dead lover, but I had thought Jenn was different.

Of course you did, I thought sourly, *because she was different to you. She counted.*

I lay there for a long moment; slowly the sound of footsteps on the deck came to me. The door opened and closed. My heart started pounding. A minute later, Jenn poked her head through the doorway and smiled at me.

"Good morning, sleepy-head. Would you like a latte?"

"I thought you'd gone," I stuttered. She looked startled.

"Gone? I left a note .... Did you just wake up?" I nodded, and looked at my watch as she laughed. It was almost noon. "You were out of milk so I went to grab some. I expected you'd be up by now."

"I ... I ...." I didn't know what to say. All of a sudden I felt on top of the world.

"What, did you think I'd run off?" I just looked at her, and she sobered, and came in and sank down on the bed beside me. Taking my hands in hers, she kissed them gently. "It'll take a lot more than last night to throw me, Kat."

The look she gave me was something more than I had expected. It lasted only a second, then a veil fell over her face and it was gone. She coughed and stood up.

"I'll make us a couple of lattes," she said, and left the room.

I took my time dressing, and joined her at the dining table. She had fixed tuna salad sandwiches and lattes, and was staring out at the golfers on the course.

"Thanks," I told her, taking a bite of my sandwich. She nodded absently. "When are your parents getting back?"

"On the four o'clock ferry. I won't be able to come over tonight. They'll expect me there." I shrugged, trying to appear nonchalant. "I have to run back up to Raleigh tomorrow. Sarah's having a problem at the gallery and I have to help her out. I'll be gone until Wednesday morning." I didn't want her to go, and I told her so. "I have to. Come with me, Katherine."

"I can't. I have to oversee the work on the house." We lapsed into silence. I stared at my sandwich, not hungry all of a sudden. *Why do I care whether she goes or not?* I didn't want to know the answer to that question. This was supposed to be a simple summer romance, no strings, no ties.

"Lynne's coming next week."

"Oh, great." I took another bite and chewed mechanically. Jenn poked at her crust and wouldn't look at me.

"This isn't because of last night."

"I didn't say it was." She looked at me, and I saw the strain on her face.

"It isn't. Will things – still be the same when I get back?"

I stared at her, trying to decipher her question.

"Do you mean us?" She nodded. "Of course!"

She seemed relieved. "I'm glad."

Strangely, I was glad too.

* * *

Monday, after waking alone and taking Jenn to an early ferry, I spent a quiet morning on the computer. I fixed lunch and ate it at the table with my free hand punching in stock figures and my eyes on the television. It seemed awfully empty, and not even the arrival of two new investment reports in the mail was enough to spark any real interest. I was preoccupied.

My cellular phone rang mid-afternoon, and I answered it knowing who it was already. "Hi, Mel."

"How's it going?"

"Fine." I picked up the remote and turned the channel to MTV, then to Nickelodeon. "How's Belinda?"

"She's fine. What's wrong? You sound distant. I'm not interrupting anything, am I?"

"No. Jenn's in Raleigh for a few days." Melissa made a sound. "I'm catching up on work."

"Are you two still ...?"

"Yes. Although why, I can't imagine." I turned the television off and stood, pacing across the room with the phone cradled to my ear.

"And what's that supposed to mean?"

I sighed and told her about my nightmare. "Any sensible woman would be out of here by now."

"You underestimate yourself, Katherine. You've made an art of picking women who will run when you want them to."

"Now, look, Mel. I'm not paying peak rates for you to lecture me on my love life."

"Then I won't. But I think you should consider this; one possible reason for the increase in your dreams is that you're finally undergoing catharsis. And I can only think of one good reason for that."

"I'm hanging up now, Melissa."

"Go ahead. Call me later." I hung up and tossed the phone onto the couch. Melissa had pushed me from merely frustrated into a full-fledged irritation. Even from three thousand miles away, she was trying to play matchmaker.

My foul humor lasted through Tuesday, which I spent in bed reading, and into Wednesday morning. Jenn had said she was arriving back on the island around noon, but I didn't expect her to contact me until later. She would have family business to attend to first. I was surprised when she knocked on my door at one. She had a box with her.

Seeing her evaporated my bad mood instantly. I unlocked the door and let her in, my arms going around her in a warm hug. She kissed me and stepped back.

"How was your trip?"

"Fine," she laughed. "I brought you something."

I took the box she held out. It was about eighteen inches square. "What is it?"

"Something from the gallery." I took it to the table and opened it, withdrawing a sculpture. It was an abstract, but obviously of two women intertwined in a moment of passion.

"It's gorgeous! How much is it?"

"It's a gift, silly." I looked at her. I'd seen work of this caliber at galleries in Seattle with price tags in the four-digit range.

"I can't accept it. It had to cost – " She held up her hand.

"I'm the owner of the gallery, remember? The artist is an up and coming, and I think it would be great if she could get some west coast exposure. Her card's in there, too, if anyone ever likes it and asks you where you got it. Now that you have a nice business-like explanation, shut up. I wanted you to have it."

"Thank you, Jenn." I didn't know what to do. No one had ever given me a gift like that. She shrugged.

"A memento of this summer." I thought I detected a faint catch in her voice, but decided I had just imagined it when I looked into her smiling face.

"I –" There. I'd almost said *I love you* again. "I'll put it somewhere safe for now." I was replacing it in the box carefully when I felt her arms around me. Turning into her embrace, I lifted my head to her kiss. It was long and tender, with just a hint of passion.

Too soon, she stepped away. "I have to go. I'll be back later tonight." I nodded, still tingling from the touch of her lips. She reached over and ran light fingers down my cheek, and was gone.

*   *   *

Friday night came and we lay in the double bed of the loft at my house. Jenn had helped me move back in that morning, after the workmen had cleared out. It was hard to believe that there had been any damage done; other than the front steps which I hadn't had replaced knowing that we'd be moving the house soon, everything looked the same.

I lay in Jenn's arms and stared at the ceiling as she murmured sweetness into my ear. The past two nights we had made love, and each night after we were done, she'd gotten up and dressed and gone home. Just like before. Just like she'd always done. And I was miserable. I wanted her to stay, wanted to wake up in the morning to the sound of her breathing.

I had talked to Melissa about it earlier in the day, while Jenn was playing golf with her mother and another mother/daughter team. Melissa had told me that I should wake up and smell the damn coffee. And as much as it went against what I thought I should be doing, I had agreed with her.

And now I lay in bed and ran my fingers down Jenn's back, feeling the goosebumps that sprang up. "Darling?"

"Yes?" I felt strangely tentative. I wasn't suggesting anything permanent, anything extreme, but my mouth was dry as though I were proposing.

"Don't go home."

"I suppose I could call ...." I raised up and looked down at her gentle face, brushing hair out of her eyes.

"No. Don't go home at all. Stay here the rest of the summer." Jenn was silent for a very long moment.

"Kat, what would I tell my parents ...." I sighed and fell back, out of her embrace.

"I don't know. Tell them I offered and you accepted. Tell them I was lonely by myself. Please, I really can't bear it for you to keep going back every night."

"I didn't know you felt that way ...." I felt something coming up in me, something making an effort to divorce my emotions from what I was saying.

"It's not that. We've only got until the end of the summer, and I don't want to waste any of that time." I swallowed hard; once again I had put a limitation on our relationship. There would be a definite end to it, and we would go on with our lives as though nothing extraordinary had happened over the summer.

"I have to think about it," she said, crossing her arms.

"Besides," I continued. "I like having you around."

She smiled at me. "I'll still have to think about it."

I nodded quietly and she slipped out of bed and strode over to the rocking chair where her clothes were. She got dressed and came back to sit on the edge of the bed. I kept looking at her, waiting for her to tell me no.

"We're playing golf tomorrow with Tracy Andrews and Margot Fuller. I'll pick you up at nine," she said. I managed a smile and nodded. I hadn't been rejected out of hand. That was something.

"That's fine." She stood again and started toward the stairs. As her foot touched the first step, she glanced back over her shoulder and winked.

"Then you can help me get my clothes together." Before I could gather myself together to respond, she was gone.

*   *   *

The next week passed in such a blur of domestic pleasure that I was certain I had died and gone to heaven. I awoke every morning in Jenn's arms, saw her smiling face across the table at breakfast, lunch and dinner, spent every night together, in pleasure and in comfort.

I dreamed about Caroline those nights, and when I came awake with the trembling, Jenn would be there, holding me. She never mentioned Caroline's name to me again, never asked about the dreams. I was thankful for her presence, her understanding.

My social obligations had been fulfilled finally, and I didn't rush to make any more, wanting to fill my days with one woman only. Jenn seemed to enjoy sitting on the deck reading, or coming in from a round of golf and watching me typing away at the computer. She respected that I had to work a little each day, and I respected that she wanted time to herself for her golf game. The Club tournament was coming up, and I was excited to think that she might well win it.

I immersed myself in the present, not allowing myself to think about the future, about the end of this pleasure. I fought to keep Caroline from my mind as well, wanting only Jenn to occupy my thoughts when I leaned over the rail of the balcony in the morning.

It was as close to love as I had allowed myself to come since Caroline. But still I couldn't take the final step that would put Jenn equal with her, couldn't say those words which would end my love for Caroline. I wouldn't say them; it would be a denial to Caroline to say I love you to anyone else, ever. I was walking a tight, thin line between happiness and madness, and occasionally I found myself wondering which side I would be on when I finally slipped and fell.

For the sake of appearances, Jenn had moved her clothes into the spare bedroom. Her parents had been a little surprised about the sudden change in arrangements, but had accepted it in good humor. Apparently, Mrs. Brooks, who was there far more than her husband who only came down three days a week, was not averse to having time alone herself.

Then came the Friday that Lynne Peterson was to arrive. I was dreading her visit, because it would mean that I wouldn't have Jenn all to myself, and because Lynne knew about Caroline. Jenn had told her parents she was not going to meet Lynne at the ferry, because she had a golf game planned. This was true, though she had arranged it specifically to coincide with her sister's arrival. Jenn, it seemed, was looking forward to the visit as little as I was.

I was spared Lynne's presence for the first three days of her visit. Fortunately, she didn't feel any pressing need to catch up. Jenn spent more time away from the house, and came back almost invariably irritated, but she took solace in my arms and relaxed soon enough. Monday morning, she left for a golf game and I went to work, thinking we might survive .

I was at the house, waiting for Jenn to get back from her game, when Lynne arrived. She came up and knocked on the back door, and I didn't recognize her at first. After all, I hadn't seen her since college.

I let her in with a vague greeting, and offered her tea. She looked quite pregnant, but I had a feeling that not all of the weight had been gained recently. Her blonde hair was touched up and I thought she wore too much makeup. In short, she looked exactly like my mother had at thirty-five. That was a terrifying thought.

"Well, sit down," I said, remembering to be the good hostess. "It's been eons, hasn't it?"

"Yes, I suppose it has," Lynne said, sinking awkwardly onto the couch. And I thought pregnant women were supposed to be beautiful. This one just looked tired.

"Ah, congratulations on everything I've missed."

"Thank you." We sat in an uncomfortable silence.

"Jenn should be back any time," I offered. Lynne nodded.

"Mother tells me you're having the house moved back after all."

- 150 -

"Yes. After that last storm I decided there were too many memories to this old place." I waited for her to bring up Caroline. There had been a brief time when the three of us had been good friends. Lynne had attended Caroline's funeral. That was the last time I'd seen her.

"Mother tells me you haven't married," Lynne said in an offhanded tone. I looked at her squarely, remembering what Jenn had said.

"No, I haven't." I might have said more, but just then Jenn came stomping in. She glowered at me, and I knew she hadn't played well. "Oh, Jenn! Look who's here."

"Great. Do we have any beer? God, I can't believe I played that crappy." She came back into the living room and collapsed across a chair, beer in hand. I shot her a tentative smile and she winked at me.

"So, ah, Lynne. Are you working?"

"I just left my position with NationsBank. I was in financial management. Peter received a promotion in his law firm, so we felt I could stay home with the baby."

"How nice for you." I wanted to gag. Lynne had turned into the sort of person we used to laugh about. She was a Yuppie. I was willing to bet she drove a BMW.

"What are you up to these days, Katie?"

"I'm self-employed," I responded. "I'm in investments."

"Why'd you stop by, Lynne?" Jenn asked all of a sudden. "Did mom make you?"

"Certainly not," Lynne replied haughtily. "I haven't seen Katie in years. I just wanted to catch up. And I wanted to see you. You've hardly been at the house since I got there. Honestly, Jennifer."

"Have you caught up? All the important questions – what're you doing, how's Seattle, are you still queer?"

"Jenn!" I exploded, coming almost out of my seat. Jenn was glaring at her sister, who was suddenly interested in the carpet.

"I saw mom on the way home. She seemed awfully interested all of a sudden in why you asked me to stay with you. Seems my dear sister asked her if she trusted me with you."

I opened my mouth to speak, then thought better of it and shut it again. No wonder Jenn was so angry looking.

"Now, Jennifer, don't take things out of proportion. I was just trying to look out for you. You're really very innocent sometimes. Look at how Sue Fleischer took advantage of you." I looked between the two, trying to figure out what was going on, if Lynne knew about Jenn. Jenn shook her head.

"You don't know a thing about what went on between me and Sue. And you don't know a thing about what's going on between me and Kat."

"I didn't come over here to argue with you, Jennifer."

"I'm sick of your bigoted attitude, Lynne. If you can't be nice, then I don't want to be around you." The two women were both on their feet, toe to toe, yelling at each other. Jenn was growing quite red in the face.

"I warned you about that girl. And she took you for every cent you had." Jenn went silent. I looked at her, but she wouldn't meet my eyes. Lynne turned to me. "I'm sorry that we had this little disagreement in front of you, Katie, but you have to understand. I'm just concerned for my little sister. She lets herself get into situations she shouldn't."

"Am I a situation, Lynne?" I couldn't help the snide tone that crept into my voice. I've been accused of many things, but this was something novel.

"You know what I'm talking about."

"I'm afraid I don't," I said evenly.

"I've heard about how chummy you've gotten with Jennifer. Mother thinks its wonderful she has someone older and more mature to look up to, but I know what's really going on."

"That's enough, Lynne," Jenn said in a low voice.

"As soon as your lover left —"

"Melissa, if that is who you are talking about, is not my lover. She's my room mate."

"Lynne, that's far enough," Jenn growled.

"Oh, Jennifer, can't you see? She's trying to get you into bed. For once open your eyes and look!" I burst out laughing. I had to. Lynne was pointing at me like I was the original predatory dyke, chasing after sweet innocent Jennifer Brooks.

"Tell me, Lynne, did you take classes to be such a jackass or did it just come with maturity?" She glared at me.

"You can't stand there and tell me you aren't a lesbian. After the way you and Caroline Dunn carried on ...."

"I'm not about to tell you I'm not a lesbian, Lynne. But I haven't been trying to seduce your sister." That was true.

"I'm sure Mother doesn't know about this. She'll have something to say about it when she finds out." Jenn stepped up beside me and put her hand on my arm.

"Mother isn't going to find out unless I tell her, Lynne. If you say one word about Katherine I swear to God I'll break your neck." Lynne looked between us.

"I'm just trying to protect you ...."

"I don't need protection," Jenn snapped. "I've known about Kat as long as you have. You're the one who's being blind and innocent. I'm a lesbian too."

Lynne stared at her. Then she stared at me.

"You ... you ...." Then she took a deep breath and looked at me in a different way, with accusation and hate in her eyes. "This is your fault."

"It is not," Jenn yelled. "It's nobody's fault that I'm gay, Lynne! I was born this way, I've always been this way and I always will be this way!"

"I think perhaps we should sit down," I suggested. "You can each have five minutes to speak your piece, without yelling, without accusing." I've gone through coming out traumas before, with clients. But never involving someone I was currently sleeping with.

"I don't need to sit down," Lynne said in a huff. "I'm leaving."

"Don't be an idiot and go screaming to mother, Lynne. I'll tell her you're being hysterical again. She doesn't want to know about me, and she won't listen."

"She might when she finds out Katherine Jenkins seduced you right under her nose."

"She didn't seduce me," Jenn said, suddenly very calm. "I seduced her. You don't think I just suddenly became a lesbian, do you? I've been sleeping with women since I was eighteen."

"I don't want to hear this."

"Well," Jenn said, warming to her subject, "you're going to. I've slept with every woman I've lived with since college. I slept with Sue Fleischer. And it isn't any of your damned business if I decide to sleep with Kat."

"Please keep me out of this," I said quietly. Jenn put her arm around my waist.

"I'm happy, Lynne. Doesn't that mean something to you? Doesn't it matter than I'm very happy the way I am?" Lynne turned up her nose.

"No. It's illegal, it's immoral .…"

"At least it's not fattening," Jenn interjected. "You've always been a pompous pain in the ass, Lynne. Go on, tell mother if you insist. But I'll never speak to you again. Now get out." Lynne turned and stomped out with as much dignity as an overweight pregnant woman can muster. I waited until she was down the stairs to collapse onto the sofa.

"Jesus H. Christ," I muttered. Jenn sank down next to me, holding her head in her hands.

"I can't believe I just did that."

"Well, sweetheart, you did. Do you think she'll tell your mother?" Jenn considered, then shook her head.

"She'll figure it would be too shocking for poor mom. But I can expect books on how to get cured for Christmas."

I stroked her hair softly and gazed out the front sliders toward the water, wondering why life had to be so damned difficult.

XII.

"Well, darling, we survived," I whispered, stroking Jenn's arm softly. We were curled together on the couch, having just finished a steak dinner in celebration of Lynne's departure earlier in the day.

"Barely," she responded, touching my hair. "Another day and I'd have had to kill her."

"Don't joke about it," I sighed. I felt worn out. The previous week had been a long one for me, what with worrying about Lynne, Jenn's near-constant irritation with her sister, and my dreams. Even taking my pills hadn't helped prevent nightly recurrences of the dreams.

I'd also seen the ghost twice, once in the morning, the other time as Jenn and I returned from an evening walk. Jenn hadn't seen her, and I'd felt foolish for asking. But at last we were alone, together, and I wanted to relax.

"Do I make you happy, Kat?" I looked over into Jenn's face, and saw something unidentifiable in it.

"Yes."

"You look so tired. Is there anything I can do?" I shrugged.

"It's been a long week, Jenn." She shifted her gaze and stared over my head. I sensed her growing distant.

"You've been spending a lot of time thinking about Caroline. Maybe it's time for me to bow out gracefully."

"No! I mean – yes, I've been thinking a lot about her, but it's just that Lynne being here and all the stress .... I don't want you to go anywhere."

"I'm glad to hear it, although I was hoping to go upstairs ...."

"As long as I can go with you." She took my hand and we went up together.

Jenn undressed me in silence, her lips busy on my neck and face. I stood still and allowed her to control the pace, until she pushed me down onto the bed and knelt on the floor with her head between my legs. I spread myself to her, feeling her mouth working up my thigh towards the raging heat of my mound. Her lips were hungry. I moaned as she claimed me, lifted my hips to her.

Gently, she entered me with her fingers, her tongue lapping at the external folds of my vulva, teasing me. I had become so accustomed to her, was so comfortable with her, that I instinctively positioned myself to best take advantage of the pleasure she gave. Slowly, she built me toward climax. Then at once I was crying out her name, clenching at the bedspread.

And abruptly, my legs closed on empty air. I opened my eyes to see her standing over me, her mouth clamped shut, a look of anger on her face. I ached from the interruption of my orgasm.

"What's wrong, Jenn?" She wiped her face on her sleeve and glared at me. "Darling?"

"Don't. How could you?" I was clueless.

"How could I what? Come?"

"No." She turned and strode across the room, toward the stairs. She hesitated, and spun back around. "When I'm making love to a woman, I'd like to hear my own name when she comes."

"What? Oh, no ...." Jenn clenched her fists.

"Caroline. I'm so god damned sick of Caroline! You dream about her, you see her on the beach, and now you're calling her name when we have sex. Why won't you let her go?"

"I'm sorry, Jenn. I'm so sorry ...." I sat up, reaching for my shirt. Jenn's shoulders slumped.

"I shouldn't have expected anything else. I knew what I was getting into. I guess I thought I might be different."

"You are different, Jenn! I can't help but think about her. Every night for the last week I've watched her drown. I don't care how it happened, I can't forget that."

"And I've watched you slowly dying in front of my eyes. Is this what happens every time you take a lover? Does Caroline come back and make sure you don't forget her? You know what, I don't blame you. I blame her!" I got up, pulling the shirt over my bare chest. Jenn's body was tense, and she backed away when I neared her.

"Jenn, please. You have to believe you're different from the others. I don't want to drive you off like this!"

"I don't care if we ever see each other again after this summer. But if we're going to have a relationship, I want you. Only you, not Caroline. So you'd better decide. Her or me." She started down the stairs.

"Where are you going?"

"To bed. In my room. Where I'll be for the rest of the summer unless you decide to leave Caroline out of our love life. Think about it." Helplessly, I watched her leave.

I couldn't believe I'd called out Caroline's name. But when I stopped and thought, I remembered doing it. Slowly, I returned to the bed. I'd finally done it; I'd let her come between me and Jenn. After trying so hard not to, I'd started the break.

Sleep didn't come easily. I went downstairs and took my pill, noticing the closed door behind which Jenn was hiding. I almost went and knocked, but couldn't bring myself to continue the confrontation. So I dragged myself back upstairs and collapsed across the bed, staring at the wall.

When I crossed from wakefulness to sleep, I don't know. But all at once I was sitting on the steps of the old walkway from the house, and Caroline was sitting beside me.

"Haven't you learned anything?" She asked, leaning back on her hands. I studied her. She was still the same, but I was different. I was me, thirty four years old and miserable.

"Caroline," I began. She shook her head.

"Do you really think we'd still be together?"

"Yes, I do." I was confused, knowing that I was dreaming, but unable to control the dream. "Of course we would be."

"You have to let me go, Katherine. Let me leave here." She swept the horizon with her arm. "I'm ready to leave."

"What do you mean?" I got up and walked down the steps to the beach. She followed a few paces behind me.

"What I mean is, you've got to release me from this place. You're keeping me here, and I'm ready to move on."

I frowned. "How am I keeping you here? I love you."

"And your love prevents me from leaving. Katherine, you have another chance at happiness, a real chance. You can't keep living in the past."

I stopped and turned to her. She seemed so pale, so young. Her eyes were hollow, but her face still held the glow of love that I remembered so well. I wanted to hold her in my arms, to never let her go, but she stepped away from me.

"Stop blaming yourself."

"I can't."

"Yes, you can. You have to. If you really love me, you'll give me leave to find my own place. I don't belong here, Katherine. I don't want to be a ghost in your life forever."

I stared at her. "What is that supposed to mean?"

"Katie," she sighed, smiling wanly, "I've never left your thoughts. Imagine if I'd lived to see what you've done with your life. How it has made me feel to see you throwing away chance after chance, knowing that I'm responsible?"

"But I'm afraid. I don't want to lose part of myself like I did with you. I gave you so much, I don't have anything left to give." She shook her head and sighed.

"And you're the psychologist. If you'd let me go, you'd find that part of you coming back. You can give it away again and again as long as you're willing to let go. You've already given Jenn more than you realize."

"How come you're so smart all of a sudden?" She laughed and looked at me as if I were a small child.

"I'm dead, Katherine. It gives one an interesting perspective. Can't you see that the part of you that you gave me, that's what's keeping me tied to this place? Take it back; let me move on to my future. And you can go on to yours."

"Caroline, darling ...."

"No. I'm not your darling any more, Katherine. Jenn is. She should be."

I woke up in a sweat as Caroline just faded out of my vision. I wasn't frightened; it hadn't been a nightmare. But I didn't know what to make of it. I lay back against the pillows and listened to the waves breaking outside the house.

If I didn't know better, I'd think I was just broken up with by a ghost. Maybe I was. And Caroline was right, I had given Jenn more of me than I'd planned to, more than I thought I could possibly give someone.

But I'm afraid. Terribly afraid. I don't know if I remember how to love. Not a real, living, day to day love. Oh, God, what am I going to do?

*   *   *

I was up early the next morning, drinking coffee and staring dully out the window at the slate gray sky. It was raining, not a downpour, but enough to dampen my already low spirits. I didn't expect Jenn up for another couple of hours, and so when she opened her door at seven thirty and padded toward the kitchen, I was so surprised I didn't know what to say. She poured herself a cup of coffee and came to the table, sitting across from me.

"Well?" Her voice was tired.

"Jenn, I'm sorry. I'm sorry I've been preoccupied. I guess Mel was right; it was a kind of catharsis. I had to get over Caroline once and for all. I think I've finally laid that ghost to rest. For her sake, I hope I have."

Jenn watched me over her cup, and I could see her face changing as she shifted through my statement. Then she took a sip of coffee and sighed.

"You're still putting her first."

"You're right. I shouldn't. After all, she's dead." I'd never said it that way. The words fell on me like bricks. That's what I'd been doing all these years, putting Caroline first. Putting her ahead of my own well-being. Putting the feelings of a dead woman ahead of my own very much alive emotions.

"And I'm not."

"No, you aren't. And I realized some time last night that I'm not either. Caroline drowned, not me. And I've been living like I did. Thanks for making me see that."

"I don't know what to say." She looked at me, obviously confused. I reached out a tentative hand and covered hers. "Kat...."

"Jenn." She didn't resist as I drew her to her feet and around the table into my arms. "This is the here and now."

"Yes," she whispered. I kissed her hands.

"You and me."

"Yes." I kissed her chin.

"Just the two of us."

"Yes." I kissed her lips.

It was like kissing her for the first time, so strong was the jolt that ran through me. And I knew then that I was kissing her for the first time. For the first time there was no one else in my thoughts as my tongue sought out hers in the moist darkness.

There was no one else in my thoughts as my hands moved up under her T-shirt, seeking the swelling softness of her breasts, claiming them. No one else but Jenn and me as I moved her backward into the room in which she had spent the night, the room in which Caroline and I had spent so many nights together.

But Caroline was not there. Only Jenn and me as I pressed her gently across the bed, pulling her shirt up, off, my mouth on her neck, her throat, her shoulders. She was moaning softly, running her fingers through my hair.

I stripped her naked, pulled my shirt off over my head with impatient hands, and joined her on the bed, taking her in my arms, pressing the length of my body against hers, feeling her skin on mine. My hands explored the planes of her shoulders, the curve of her back, the softness of her hips. Our lips touched again, melded, tongues dancing with each other.

I tasted her breasts on my lips, suckled at her hardened nipples, and thought only of her. I moved down her body, reveling in the feel of her, the scent of her, the taste of her, my mouth claiming her wetness, spreading her lips and lapping at her with long, patient strokes.

Never before had I been so totally consumed with making love to a woman, never had I experienced the hunger with which I took her. Her moaning became louder, more insistent, her hands knotted into my hair, her head turning back and forth in a spastic rhythm.

I filled her with my tongue, drank of the waves of wetness flowing from her, then returned to her hardened clitoris with my teeth and lips, my fingers slipping into her. Her hips thrust forward to meet my hand, rocking urgently, almost violently, against me.

Then the sudden stillness preceding climax, and she went with a long scream into a spasming orgasm as I pressed into her, my mouth against her. When she collapsed back across the mattress I moved up her body and gathered her into my arms, kissing her as I pressed my own hips against hers, experiencing a new height of arousal.

"Tell me what you want," Jenn breathed around the kiss, her hands on my waist. I guided her hand between my legs and showed her how I wanted her fingers, then slipped up so that I sat astride her waist and offered my breasts to her mouth. She suckled at me and took me as I had shown her. I moved with her into a quick, explosive climax, then rolled over so that she was on top of me and spread my legs.

"Again," I ordered. I was hungry, wild with need. I'd never felt so demanding, so insistent. We made love repeatedly, until neither of us could move. Then we slept again.

Caroline was nowhere to be found.

*   *   *

The next month brought a change in our relationship that I could never have expected, would have thought impossible just a short time before. I found myself growing closer and closer to Jenn with each passing day, every morning awakening to her face and thinking that we could become no more united, and each night falling asleep knowing that we had.

Jenn took third place in her flight at the ladies club tournament, and proudly showed off her silver tray to me, and I responded with an enthusiasm I had forgotten I possessed. It pleased me to see her so happy. And when I made a series of good moves in the market, netting myself a tidy profit – enough to cover the cost of the repair work on the house – Jenn treated me to dinner complete with champagne and flowers.

It occurred to me that there might be rumors starting about us, but I didn't care. It was all so new to me, this state of rapture that

I was tempted to shout it from the very top of the lighthouse; I was happy and I didn't care who knew it.

Somewhere in the back of my mind, I knew that there was a chance I was going overboard, that I was giving more of myself away than I should, more than Jenn would ever return. As the summer lengthened, the days grew longer and hotter, and we began to daily remind each other that soon it would be over.

This wasn't done in so many words, but phrases began to creep into our conversations, phrases such as "When I go back to Seattle ... " and "After this, Raleigh will seem dull ...." And every time I said something, I felt my heart give a disquieting wrench, and I wanted to cry out, to hold her and not let the next day come, the day that would bring us one step closer to the end.

One night, as we sat on the deck after dinner, Jenn with a glass of wine and I with a Coke, she leaned back and looked at the sky for a long moment before turning her face to me.

"This hasn't been too bad for a summer romance, has it?"

"No, darling, it hasn't." I met her gaze and saw the same unidentifiable something that had been there on so many other occasions. As always, it was gone almost as soon as I saw it.

"We weren't too old?"

"No, Jenn, we aren't." She nodded, closed her eyes, and that was the end of it.

I knew, of course, that there would have to be an end. The summer could not last forever, and Jenn had a business to run. She made several trips back to Raleigh during the month, usually gone overnight. On those nights I would stand on the upper balcony for hours, watching the stars and wondering at the change that had come over my life.

Could this really be me, this woman who waited for her lover to return with a desire so great that it drowned out even my desire for independence? What had happened to me that I was so willing to surrender parts of myself to Jenn that I had kept under tight lock and key for so long?

And the end finally arrived. August was half over and the Brooks' were packing to return to Winston-Salem. Jenn had to get back to Raleigh in time for a series of showings scheduled to coincide with the opening of the fall term at the colleges. And I had to get ready for the task of having the house moved.

Neither of us spoke of it for almost a week, but every night as we made love, it became a little more strained, a little more desperate. And I knew why that was.

I didn't want her to leave.

* * *

It was the night before Jenn was to go. Her bags were packed, waiting to be taken to the ferry the next morning. We had fixed a quiet dinner and were eating on the deck, under the stars and a bright full moon. Jenn was unusually quiet, and I picked at my food without much interest. Finally, the silence became too much for me. I pushed back my chair and stood up.

"This is where you walk away, right?" Jenn was staring at her plate. I looked down at the top of her head and sighed.

"According to the script, yes."

"I don't like your script." Her words were so soft I almost didn't hear them. I didn't know how to respond.

"Neither do I," I said finally. She stood up and came to me, putting her arms around me and pulling me close.

"Katherine, there's something I have to talk to you about. I've been needing to tell you this for a long time." I didn't want to hear what she was going to say. I was certain she could see how I felt, was trying to gently remind me what we'd agreed to.

"Jenn, don't. I can't bear to hear it." I broke away and turned to the railing. Behind me, I heard her breathing.

"I have to. Kat, I know we agreed ...."

"Yes. We agreed. I can't help how I feel." She gave a little half-sob and I turned. There were tears in her eyes. "What ...?"

- 165 -

"Neither can I, Kat. I love you."

"In the name of God, why?" I was so dumb-founded that I asked before I could stop myself.

"At first, because I knew how much you loved Caroline. I'd never met a woman with that much passion. Then as I got to know you, got to watch you …. You were like the sea the night of the storm. Wild; you'd been hurt so badly that you were still lashing out this long after. I wanted to comfort you, to make you forget her."

"You pitied me." My voice was flat. Jenn shook her head.

"Never. I saw strength in you. I – I guess I was selfish. I wanted you to love me the way you loved Caroline. I've never known that kind of devotion." She was crying, silently. Her voice was choked, but she controlled herself. "I didn't mean to fall in love with you. I'm sorry …."

I took a step forward. "There's nothing to be sorry about," I started. She shook her head.

"I know it's foolish. I'm making a fool out of myself."

"You can't love me, Jenn. You just can't." My words sprang from disbelief. "It's so impossible …."

My mind was whirling with how impossible it was; we lived on opposite sides of the country. We had our own separate lives, jobs. I could no more up and move to Raleigh than she could to Seattle.

"I do. I love you so much it hurts me, Katherine."

"Oh, God …." I wanted to hold her. "Jenn, I don't know what to say …."

Her face was streaked with tears, her eyes wide. "Say you love me too."

Yes, I agreed mentally, *say you love her. Say what you feel.*

"I – I …." She was backing away from me. I felt a swirl of confusion. "Jenn …."

"Oh, how could I have let this happen? Damn, damn, damn!" Before I could stop her, she spun and dashed into the house, out the back door. I called after her, but she wouldn't answer me.

I heard the sound of the golf cart as she drove away. I dropped into my chair and put my head in my hands.

"Oh, Jenn," I whispered to the ocean. "I love you too."

*　*　*

I sat on the deck for an hour, staring at the moon. Then I went and called the Brooks' house. Mrs. Brooks informed me that Jenn didn't want to talk to me and that she'd be by in the morning to collect her bags.

I could tell from the tone in Mrs. Brooks' voice that she held me accountable for whatever had caused Jenn to come home in the state I knew she had to be in.

I sank onto the sofa, feeling a dull ache in my heart. Why hadn't I been able to respond with the words I knew I felt? What had prevented me from revealing the true reason I hadn't wanted to hear what Jenn was saying, that I was afraid she was going to tell me it was over and I had to accept that?

A million questions filled my thoughts, none with easy answers. I began to feel a headache behind my eyes. I wanted to cry. Did it make a difference that she loved me back? Suddenly, things I had not allowed myself to dream were possible.

Had I been unable to respond because of the fear that something real and intimate had come out of our relationship? That I didn't want her to go, not just for now, but for always?

Was I watching another drowning, the drowning of love?

I didn't sleep at all well that night, and was up before dawn, pacing the living room. When Jenn arrived for her bags, I would have to talk to her, have to convince her to stay with me. I couldn't leave it like this, not now.

She arrived at eight, with her mother in tow. I frowned when I saw the elder woman at the door, but let them in. Jenn wouldn't look at me, but her mother stood there glaring.

"Jenn, I need to talk to you," I said. Jenn shook her head. "Please. It's important."

"I think it was all said last night." Her voice was a whisper. I glanced back at Mrs. Brooks, standing with her arms crossed and looking fierce.

"No, it wasn't. I'll say it right here if I have to." That shook Jenn into looking at my face. I saw the circles under her eyes, the redness running through them. It tore at my heart.

"All right. In here." She gestured to the bedroom. I followed her inside and shut the door.

"Jenn, you didn't let me finish last night."

"I couldn't take any more." Her shoulders slumped.

"You know I couldn't move back here. I can't hide like that any more. I've been out too long. This summer has almost killed me." I was trying to reason with her. Why in the hell was I doing that? All I really needed to say were those three simple words.

"I know."

"Jenn, look at me." I searched her face. She looked defeated, tired and old. And I was responsible. "Oh, Jenn. I haven't said I love you in fourteen years. You couldn't expect me to just pop out with it on command, could you?"

"No, I suppose not. It's just .... We got on so well together this summer. It seemed so real ...." I sighed and reached for her hands. She allowed me to take them.

"It was real, Jenn. A lot more real than I expected, more real than I was ready for. I told you I wasn't ready for a long term relationship." She nodded, looking away. I saw tears starting to form in her eyes. "Don't cry. Please don't do that."

"I don't care about a long term relationship, Kat. I just wanted you to care for me like I did for you." I gazed at her, hoping my face was encouraging, and smiled.

"Darling, I do." *Just say it and stop fighting.* "I – stay with me. Just a little longer."

She shook her head. "I can't. It hurts too much."

"I don't want to hurt you, Jenn. I love you." The words just came out, as easily as if I'd been saying them forever. And once I'd said them, and I saw the look of shocked amazement on her face, I drew her to me and kissed them all over her face. "I love you, I love you. I've loved you for so long."

"But .... Last night ...."

"I misunderstood what you were trying to say until it was too late, darling. I was too busy trying to tell you myself." She smiled at me.

"Oh, Katherine."

"Stay with me. Please. Tell your mother to go without you."

"Kat .... Yes, all right." She kissed me softly, then opened the door and walked out with me behind her. Her mother was still standing by the door, looking at her watch.

"It's about time, Jennifer. We're going to miss the ferry if you don't hurry up. What are you smiling about?" Jenn glanced up at me.

"You go on, Mother. I've decided to stay here a little longer."

"What on earth is going on here, Jennifer Brooks? One minute you're crying and cursing and telling me you don't ever want to speak to Katherine Jenkins again and the next you're staying longer? I don't understand you at all." Jenn slipped up next to me, putting her arm around my waist.

"Mother, do you remember Lynne talking about Kat and Caroline Dunn?" Mrs. Brooks frowned, looked puzzled.

"Well, yes. I don't see why she had to bring that up, it happening so long ago .... Why?" I looked up at Jenn, sensing what she was about to do and not quite understanding why.

"I'm staying, Mother, because ... because I love Katherine. And she loves me. And that leaves us a lot to talk about."

Mrs. Brooks froze. She looked at Jenn.

She looked at me.

She looked at Jenn's arm, comfortable around my waist.

"Oh." She opened her mouth to say more.

"You're going to miss your ferry. We'll talk about this when I get back to Raleigh. I know you're going to have a lot of questions."

Mrs. Brooks raised one arched eyebrow. "I have only one question, Jennifer. Have you totally lost your mind?"

"No, Mother, I haven't. Now, please, leave." I disentangled myself from Jenn and walked to the door, pushing it open.

"Have a safe drive home, Mrs. Brooks," I said, fighting to remain calm. She hesitated.

"Good bye, Mother." Jenn moved to take her mother's elbow and guide her to the door.

"Your father and I will have something to say about this."

"I'm sure you will," Jenn said, and closed the door. I watched through the glass as her mother walked numbly down the stairs.

"Jenn, I'm not sure that was a wise thing to do."

"I had to."

"Do you realize how hard it's going to be for you now?" She nodded, and held out her hands to me. I took them, stepping close into her. She kissed me, her mouth soft on mine, quietly insistent.

She led me upstairs, to the bed, pulled me down onto it so that we lay side by side, our faces close. Jenn reached out and caressed my cheek.

"Do you really love me?"

"I wouldn't have said it if I didn't, darling. I love you desperately."

"Show me."

I kissed her again, my hands on her body, undressing her. As I had started to do before, I said I love you to every part of her, gently, with a tenderness that I hoped would underscore the words. She responded to me in a way that I had not seen before, giving herself to me with a surrender that left me feeling honored to have been the recipient of her passion.

We lay together afterwards, touching each other with familiar caresses. I knew her body, every line and curve and plane, and ran my fingers along the parts I could reach with a sense of pleasure at that knowledge, at the thought that she had trusted me with the things that made her feel good, the ways to bring her to the greatest pleasure.

We had truly shared something beyond the sex that I had known for so many years from women who's faces were now hard to recall, who's bodies were all as one, whom I could pass on the street or meet at a bar without the slightest twinge of renewed desire.

No matter if Jenn and I parted that night, if we never shared this intimacy again, I knew that I would feel exactly the same if we ever met again as I did at that moment, that if she came to me in a year, or five, or ten, I would open my arms and my heart to the feelings that would simply have been hidden, but would never – could never – be extinguished.

I felt her in my arms, felt a sudden overpowering surge of the love I could now admit, and told her again, "I love you, Jenn."

"And I love you."

"But I still think you shouldn't have come out to your mother like that ...." I tried not to sound judgmental.

"I did it for me, Kat." She pillowed her head against me and hid her face. "I couldn't stand the thought of driving home to Raleigh, back to that hidden life. I spent last night thinking about my apartment, and I dreaded the emptiness it would have for me."

"But I know how it is when your parents know; it can be so difficult. Especially when you live so close to them." She gave a little shrug.

"I'd decided to leave the south anyway. I want to work at my art more and spend less time running a gallery for other people's efforts. I might even get back into sculpture." I rolled away, looking down at her in disbelief, studying her eyes.

"Where will you go?"

She shrugged again. "I don't know. San Francisco, maybe Portland. They both have decent-sized gay communities. And I know people in both places, I have an entrée if I decide to open another gallery."

"Why not Seattle?" She gave me an odd look, and I realized that she had accepted my love with the understanding that I wasn't ready for a relationship. I wasn't even certain what I was asking of her, only that I had to have her near me always. "You could stay with me."

"Don't you think that would be ... awkward? You already live with Melissa."

"Mel's talking about moving in with Belinda. And it's a big house. There's plenty of room for a studio in the basement or the garage, and Ballard's a very gay-friendly area .... You could open a gallery there, bring in art from the east coast ...." I bit my upper lip and studied her face. I only knew that I couldn't let her go; now that I had admitted my love, I didn't want it to end.

"I don't know ...."

"I don't want to lose you, Jenn."

"Katherine, I can't accept just friendship from you after what we've shared. I have to end it now, so that I know it's over, for my own sanity. I have to have closure."

So she still thought that I was saying good-bye, that I had closed the door on our relationship and was offering a pale imitation of what we had had. I felt giddy as I answered her, giddy with the prospect of a new life, of a new birth for myself and for us. "I'm not offering just friendship. I'm offering myself."

She sat up and stared at me. I waited, with bated breath, for her answer. She was as skittish as I about the idea of a commitment, had been hurt far more often and more frequently than I, and there was a chance ....

"You've told me about the others, Katherine, how you left them when it got too serious. I don't know that I want to wait around with my heart exposed for you to decide I'm no different."

"But you are different, Jenn. I've never asked a woman to live with me. It's already serious between us, far more serious than I ever dreamed it would be. But I love you, and I want you to come home with me, to stay with me." My voice was earnest, and I held out my hands to her to emphasize my honesty.

"For how long, Kat? How long would I be welcome in your home, your bed?"

I took her hands in mine and drew her down to me so that I could whisper the answer into her hair, "For as long as you'll have me, darling. For the rest of your life."

The only words to pass between us after that were the soft sounds of mutual desire as we made slow, gentle love, as we once again shared the intimacies that I had thought I would never experience again, that I would never want.

And then, as the morning progressed into afternoon, we wrapped our naked bodies in the bedsheets and went out onto the balcony, into the brilliance of the August sun, to plan our new life, together.